Ignition Point

A Newman Fire Dept Novella

Rae Fields

HEA Books LLC

Developmental and Line Editing: Jessica Snyder, HEA Author Services

Copyediting and Proofreading: Marie Edits

Cover design: Kari March

www.raefields.com

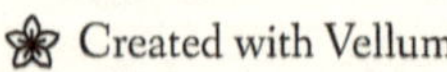 Created with Vellum

For you.
For doing the scary thing, taking a chance, and chasing a dream.

Chapter 1

Mike

Funny how your life could turn in an instant.

I climbed the front steps of a revitalized antebellum home, ready to end my day of building inspections and paperwork. As with many of the old houses in the area, this one had been renovated and rezoned as commercial property.

The Blue Lotus Yoga Studio was my last stop. And while I enjoyed this hodgepodge role of pre-fire planning and building/fire inspections that broke up my usual day on duty, I was sick and damn tired of doing most of the legwork. My counterpart was supposed to handle this building, but he'd slacked off and now we were behind.

I grabbed the door handle and turned, but the solid wood door stuck the slightest bit. I put a little muscle, and my frustration with my partner, into it and the door swung free. A startled yelp came from the other side as the door went crashing into whoever was there.

Rushing in, I found a woman teetering on a ladder. I reached her as she lost her battle with gravity and caught her tipping to the side. As I did, a small package clattered to the floor. Her chest hit mine and my arms instinctively wrapped around her petite body.

"Oof," she gasped as our bodies connected.

"I'm so sorry. I didn't expect anyone on the other side when I barged in. Are you okay?" Finally glancing down, I realized that the prettiest woman I'd ever laid eyes on was in my arms and every inch of her torso was pressed into mine. All my frustrations leaked away in an instant, along with my ability to speak.

She was fresh-faced, without a hint of makeup on, skin glowing as if she were bathed in her own ray of light. Beautiful hazel eyes, wide with alarm, stared back at me. Her mouth dropped open, showing lush lips that invited exploration. I was immediately aware that I still had her in my arms, and every place that her soft skin touched mine tingled. And I was on the job.

I released her, my hands itching to linger as she righted herself.

"Thank you."

Her voice was like honey–dripping with southern charm, sweet and a little husky.

I wanted to taste it.

She had a head-full of unruly dark blonde hair piled high in a bun. A thin sweater draped over her shoulders but left the curve of her neck exposed, begging for a kiss. A long string of tiny lights trailed behind her, half attached to the wall above and tangled in the ladder behind her.

It'd been a very long time since I'd been this drawn to a woman at first sight. I swallowed and tried to speak, only to have it come out as a croak.

On my second attempt I managed to get out, "Hi, I'm

Officer Mike Harrison. Sorry I sent you sprawling, barging in like that."

She stepped away, untangling the lights. "I was trying to finish these lights before my next class. I should've locked the door, or at least been expecting it to open."

"Can I help?"

What in the hell was I thinking? I was on the job. I didn't need to be doing chores right now. But I wanted to help her, and I lived by the Serve-and-Protect motto. So, technically, hanging a strand of lights wasn't out of my wheelhouse.

"If you wouldn't mind. That last section was a bit of a struggle for me. I can't get the little hanger tab high enough." She bent, picked up the package that had fallen to the floor and handed me a plastic temporary wall-hanger.

I took the tab and lights, and quickly finished the job for her.

"Can I put this ladder away for you?" I asked, folding it and leaning it against a wall out of the way.

"No, that's okay. I can get it."

God, that voice.

She walked into a reception area to a tall podium-like desk. I followed like a lovesick pup.

A scent in the air welcomed me, drew me in. It was something citrusy and a little earthy, but I couldn't tell if it was this intriguing woman or the little glowing orb behind her that emitted steam. I stepped closer to her and inhaled slowly. *Don't be a creeper*.

She turned to check me out, eyes widening as her gaze traveled down my body.

I worked hard to keep in shape, and I knew what I had. My chest puffed out a little as she met my gaze, a blush tinting her cheeks with a soft pink glow.

"M-May I help you, Officer?"

And yeah, I was in already. My dick stirred, making my snug uniform pants tighter. I drank her in as she did me, gripping my ballistic vest, making sure my tats and biceps bulged.

"I'm here to do a pre-fire plan walk-through and inspection." *And maybe inspect you while I'm at it.* And that was probably the lamest come-on I'd ever thought up. But damn, this woman...

She frowned. "They send the police to do that?"

I wanted to press my lips to that V on her forehead.

And where in the fuck had that thought come from? Never in my life had I even thought about kissing a woman's forehead. Still, I couldn't drag my eyes from her, so I gave myself a mental headshake and stepped closer, offering my hand.

"Sorry. Let's start over. I'm Mike Harrison with Newman Police Department. I'm on a special task force that works jointly with both the police and fire departments doing fire investigations, pre-fire planning, and inspections. The business next door had a fire recently and we noticed we didn't have your business on file. I need to do a walk-through and document a pre-fire plan."

As she slipped her hand into mine, her frown morphed to a beautiful smile. "Hi, Mike. I'm Leah Miller, co-owner of the studio." And I was lost. With just a smile, I was all in for this slip of a woman. Tingles of electricity shot up my arm, with just a single touch of her hand.

"And yes, I'd heard about the fire." She tucked an errant strand of hair behind her ear and glanced away shyly. As if, maybe, I was affecting her as well.

Behind me, the bell on the front door jingled and feminine voices filled the front hall.

"Is now a good time?" I asked. This was my last stop of the day. Before I'd walked in, I'd been ready for my day to be done. But now, I wanted to linger.

She glanced at the tablet on the counter in front of her. "Yes, we have a class starting soon, but feel free to look around."

The studio was built in a renovated older home, much like the other businesses on this side of town. Newman, situated just outside Atlanta, was a small town experiencing large growth. Big enough to have some choices in dining and entertainment, small enough that you still knew just about everyone in town.

"How long have you guys been here?" I asked. That I hadn't met this woman before told me I'd spent too much time on duty in my patrol car, and not enough time out actually meeting my citizens.

"We've been open about a year."

Impressive. And brave. Opening a yoga studio in this small town couldn't have been easy. Yet a steady stream of people walked through the door.

"Looks like business is going well," I remarked, glancing around the lobby. I'd never been this awkward talking to a woman. Maybe it was her direct gaze. Maybe it was how I couldn't look away from her pretty face, even though I knew I shouldn't stare. But something about this woman had me all unsettled.

The spacious lobby had white walls, old hardwood floors, and high ceilings. Other than vibrant green plants sitting in every corner and hanging in the window in crocheted baskets, the place had minimal décor. A bench seat with cubbies underneath ran the length of one wall under a window where the late afternoon sun streamed in, leaving a swath of light across the well-worn floor. One point of entry into the room and no cameras, but at least they had a sprinkler system.

I wandered over to a closed-off fireplace on the opposite wall and knelt in front of the old unit.

"Are you guys using the fireplace?" I called out, mainly so I could get another shot of that honeyed voice.

"No, the building was converted to central heat and air before we moved in, and I guess the owner had the fireplace boarded up. We just decorated around it."

She was right behind me. I glanced over my shoulder to find her lithe figure leaned against the doorframe of the lobby, and from the way her cheeks reddened, maybe I'd caught her checking out my ass.

Flowing pants that gathered at the ankle, with slits up the sides, teased a glimpse of skin as she crossed her legs. Her thin sweater folded across her chest, hinting a shadow of a sports bra underneath. That hair piled on top of her head, with tendrils framing her face, begged for me to bury my hands in it. My body responded to hers in a way I'd never experienced. I wanted her.

"Alarm system?" My voice got deeper each time I tried to talk to her. I had to get a grip on this lust. I was a professional, dammit.

She nodded. "Yes, wired for entry and fire detection."

The bell at the front door rang and she went to greet another newcomer. It took everything I had to turn away from her. But I didn't need to see her to eavesdrop on her conversation, relishing that sexy voice and noting the friendly way she treated each person.

These were her friends, her people, and they all seemed to love her.

From the corner of my eye, I caught her releasing her hair from its bun and redoing it as she chatted with one of her students about the upcoming class. I forced away the image of what that glorious hair would look like draped across my pillow and tried to focus on the job.

I made my way through the building, checked the breaker boxes and ticked off my inspection list, taking my time while trying to find a slick way to ask her out. Occasionally, I'd catch the sound of her laughter, or the soft tones of her response to her clients. A shocked sound drifted down the hall and caught my attention, but nothing followed, so I let it go.

She had to be all kinds of savvy to run a business and make it successful in this town. I mean, in a bigger city you'd expect to have a dedicated yoga studio. But here? Where we'd only gotten a movie theater a few years ago? And where only the who's-who were truly successful? Yeah. She was smart and dedicated.

Eventually, I completed the inspection and made my way back to the front office. Leah stood behind the counter again, frowning at her computer. Now was my chance to make a move.

"I'm done for now."

She jumped at the sound of my voice.

"Oh, I'm sorry. I forgot you were here."

Well, damn. Shot down before I even made my move. Here I was trying to find ways to get to know her better, and she'd already forgotten me. So much for the earth-shattering collision of molecules I thought we'd both felt.

I'd had a photo in the annual public safety calendar for the last three years, and maybe my ego had grown a bit prouder of that than I'd realized, considering she just deflated it with a few simple words.

Stung by her dismissal, and the fact that it affected me

so much, I didn't stop my interrogation voice from slipping in.

"Right," I clipped. "I'll write up my report and be in touch with you next week."

I placed a business card on the desk and walked away from the most beautiful woman I'd ever met.

Chapter 2

Mike

Back at the police station, I finished typing up my report and saved it, then printed a copy to take down to the Captain. I could've just emailed it, and probably would end up needing to anyway. But at the moment, my ego was suffering over being dissed so effortlessly. I hated feeling invisible and I needed to walk off that frustration. Besides, I was hoping that seeing my friends could shift me out of my shitty mood.

The newly-completed firehouse was clean and smelled of fresh paint. A row of black recliners lined up in front of a size-Outrageous television hanging on the wall. To the right of the room was a basic kitchen setup and to the left a small pool table. I passed these and headed into the hall, looking for the crew.

"Yo! Harrison, what's up?" Big Mo called from the weight bench as I walked by the workout room. He had an impressive amount of weight on the bar. His huge hands gripped tighter, and his arms bulged as he performed another rep. The man was built like a tree.

"Nothing much. Just dropping off some reports. Thoren here?"

"In here," came Thoren's voice from further inside.

The city had spared no expense when they'd built the new fire station, issuing state-of-the-art fire equipment, providing living spaces that were actually comfortable, and tricking out the gym.

I stepped forward to find my buddies. Thoren was on the universal squat machine, while Nate rode a stationary bike.

"What's up, Mikey?" Nate taunted.

"Don't fucking call me that, California." I glared at him.

He sat back with a shit-eating grin, holding his hands up in surrender.

For a half-second, I envied the firefighters' facility and their easy camaraderie. The police department had a workout room, sure. And we got to hang out at times. But for the most part, mine was a solitary job. No partner and a lot of hours alone in my patrol car. I had friends on the force, but none like these guys.

Thoren and I shared a hire date and had met during orientation with the city. For years he'd been stationed at the firehouse next to police headquarters, and from there our friendship had grown. In those early years, we'd have cookouts and battle each other in Police vs. Fire games. Then the PD headquarters moved, and Thoren and the guys relocated to their new station.

And yeah. I was just feeling feelings and I didn't like it.

I folded the papers and propped a shoulder in the doorway. I didn't know what was making me so friggin' emotional and needy, but suddenly I didn't want to go home to my empty place.

"Nothing much, just dropping a report off from an

inspection." I tapped the report against my leg. Restless. Uncomfortable.

"Did something happen with it? Cause you look kinda... off." Thoren knew me better than most anyone. That he could read that I was having a shit day meant I wasn't doing a good enough job of keeping my thoughts contained.

Thoughts of a certain yoga teacher I thought I'd had a connection with but who blew me off.

"Nah. It's nothing."

Big Mo sat up from the bench, Thoren racked his bar, and both men turned their full attention on me.

"Doesn't look like nothing," Thoren said, wiping a towel across his face.

"Eh. It's just this woman I met today." I waved off their concern.

"A woman, huh? What happened? She go crazy on you?" Nate teased, still pedaling the stationary bike, a grin on his stupid, golden-boy face.

"No, she didn't do anything. That's the problem." The words were out before I could stop them.

The three of them watched me warily until Thoren spoke up. "Why don't you tell us what happened from the beginning? I think I'm missing something."

I launched into a recap of walking into the studio and being stunned by the sight of her. Of how she basically ignored me in the end. And how, now, I couldn't get her out of my head.

"Aw, poor Mikey. What's the matter? She didn't fall head-over-heels for you the moment she laid eyes on you?" Big Mo fluttered his eyelashes at me. What a ridiculous expression on the face of a grown-ass giant of a man.

"No. Actually, she just...dissed me." It fucking sucked to admit how much that shit affected me.

"You didn't hit her with the epic Harrison double flex?" Mo flexed his huge biceps, the dark skin stretching taught over his extra-large muscles, and winked at me.

"Don't be dumb. I don't do that."

"Yes, you do," all three responded in unison.

"Fuck y'all. I do not."

Nate laughed outright from the bike, the steady rhythm of his pedaling providing a low background hum. "Yes, you do. It's not some outrageous move like Mo just made. But you do flex when you're around a hot chick."

I flipped him a bird. But he was totally right. I did flex. I worked hard to keep in shape. So what if I wanted some appreciation for it?

"What's so special about this girl?" Thoren asked. He knew I didn't get wound up like this.

"I don't know. She's just... And the way she looked at me...felt like my bones shifted or something." I lifted my hands, at a loss as to how to explain myself correctly.

Mo and Nate wore twin expressions of shock, but Thoren didn't miss a beat.

"What are you gonna do about it?"

I folded the damn report again. Twisting it into a little paper tube. I'd have to trash this one and email it after all.

"Nothing. She wasn't interested." Saying it out loud made it more real.

Thoren crossed his arms across his chest. "That's never stopped you before."

He was right, of course. But I still had this weird feeling. Like, time had stood still for me, but not for her. And those thoughts had me feeling all kinds of foolish. Every slick move I'd ever played to get a woman before just felt... useless. Cheap.

"This time is different."

Big Mo grunted, folding his beefy arms over his mountainous chest. "You need to man up. The Mike I know doesn't give up that easy. You've got to get back over there and let her know you're interested. If she's all you say she is, you might have to do more than just flex those pretty muscles. You might have to work to impress her."

I pushed off the wall and paced, gripping the back of my neck. What he suggested meant setting myself up for rejection. "What, just walk up to her and tell her I think she's the most beautiful woman I've ever laid eyes on, and I want to get to know her?"

He nodded. "Absolutely. The best way to get her attention is with some good old-fashioned honesty. If she's meant to be yours, it'll work out."

I trusted Big Mo. Of the four of us, he was the only one with any relationship history. The man had been married to a pistol of a woman for as long as I'd known him. But they seemed happy, so I had to trust that he somewhat knew what he was talking about.

I nodded at his suggestion, trying to scheme up a reason to go back to the yoga studio. Hell. According to Mo, I should just go just because I wanted to see her.

What would she do if I just waltzed into her studio and declared myself?

If I were her, I'd run the other way if some idiot came around spouting about having the feels after one meet. I wasn't too keen on the idea of getting shot down again, but I also didn't like to lose. Therefore, I needed a reason.

"What's that you've got there?" Thoren motioned to my rolled-up report.

"It's just the report from the inspection I did today."

"Don't you have some follow-up items to go over? With her?" He eyed me expectantly.

"I guess..."

Thoren grabbed the report and looked over it. Then shoved it back at me.

"You need to go check the breaker."

"I checked that."

"Check it again," he ordered then grinned. "Unless you want me to go check it out with the other guy that's doing inspections. What's his name? Jimmy? Timmy?"

The police department had assigned just two of us to the fire inspection task force, making it more of a team than a force. And the other guy was a shrimpy little shithead know-it-all who was five-foot-two with a ten-foot-tall atti-tude. No way was he getting anywhere near my pretty yoga teacher.

I snatched my report back, glaring at my best friend. "Fuck that. I do my own work." And I'd get my own woman, without competition.

I hoped.

Chapter 3

Leah

I'd been so incredibly rude to the handsome cop that came to inspect the studio.

After a restless night of dreaming about a pair of warm chocolate eyes, I woke up feeling all hot and bothered. I'd noticed how he'd looked at me with interest. I'd also noticed the ass that filled out those uniform pants perfectly. If I'd been on my game, I would've paid more attention before he left. I would've said something flirty. Been more interesting.

It wasn't in my nature to fixate on another person, but I'd been thinking about this man since the moment he left the studio yesterday.

Unsettled, I cut my morning meditation short. I couldn't focus so I headed to work and reached the studio a good hour before normal, hoping to intercept my business partner and best friend Kylie to get her help in sorting out my issue about this guy. Luckily, I found her in the back office going over the financials. I dropped my bag in my chair and tossed my phone and keys to my desk. Financial work at seven in the morning didn't appeal to me in the slightest, but we had to get the work done when we could.

"What's this card? Who is Mike Harrison, and why were the cops here?" She hit me with a barrage of questions before I could even mutter hello.

Crap. I forgot he'd left his card.

"Remember when the building next door caught on fire? He was just stopping by to do an inspection to make sure ours was sound."

"That's a little ridiculous given that we've been in here since the fire happened, right?" Kylie arched a brow at me.

"Well, now that you mention it, yes. I didn't think about it much at the time." I'd been overly distracted. "I had a little upset right after he showed."

"What happened?"

Instantly my mind replayed how I'd barged in on one of our regular students changing in the bathroom. Karen had been mid-change, struggling to get into her workout shirt. She'd turned to hide from me, but not before I noticed the kaleidoscope of color across her midriff.

"I tripped going down some stairs taking the puppy out," she'd said. I didn't believe her for a minute. I was no expert on bruises, but I knew enough to know that kind of color only came from some serious trauma.

"Are you okay?" I'd wanted to reach for her. I'd wanted to offer her assistance of some kind, but her hard glare stopped me.

"I'm fine. Really." She tried for a smile that didn't reach her eyes. "But I would appreciate your discretion," she murmured. "People have made incorrect assumptions."

I'd assured her I'd keep it to myself and walked out feeling helpless.

That day in class, she'd been stiff and tense during the

whole session, despite me altering my planned poses to make it easier for her. It made matters worse that her husband owned our building and was our landlord.

I felt guilty even contemplating sharing my thoughts with Kylie when Karen had asked me to keep it between us. But Kylie was my business partner, and she'd have a vested interest in making sure our clients were safe. Then again, what if Karen's story was legit? What if she really did trip down some stairs chasing after her puppy? I didn't need to be putting words in her mouth in a situation that was really none of my business, no matter how concerned I was, not to mention what could happen with our lease if my assumptions were wrong.

I opted for vague. "I walked in on a client changing clothes in the bathroom." I gave a little laugh, trying to make light of the heavy situation.

"Oh damn!" Kylie burst out laughing. "That had to suck. And I want to hear about that, but first, what did the cop say? And why was a cop doing the investigation? I thought that was usually the fire department. Also was he young? Good-looking?" Incorrigible as always, she waggled her eyebrows on the last question.

Yes, he'd most definitely been good-looking. The way he filled out that uniform shirt, the tattoo that peeked from the edge of his sleeve. The way his hips rolled as he walked, those handcuffs on his belt swaying with the movement. I finally admitted to myself that I'd totally checked out the way his pants cupped his butt and had gotten busted in the process. The view as he'd walked down the hall had been spectacular.

"Wow, your face just turned bright red. He must've been some kind of dude to make you blush like that."

"He made an impression. But I totally blew it." I sighed in exasperation. "As usual."

"I'm sure you didn't."

"No, I totally did. I was so distracted by walking in on Karen, I kinda flubbed the opportunity." I gulped. I'd almost said too much.

Kylie grimaced. "Oh, Karen! Awkward. She's buttoned up so tight, I bet you were both mortified."

I suddenly had an idea of why Karen seemed uptight. The woman had secrets.

"Anyway, you've got his card. Give him a call." She flicked her wrist towards me, holding said card between her fingers.

I hesitated. "I don't know." The thought of seeing him again sent a little thrill through me, but I'd always been awkward and had never been one that could make the first move. To call him out of the blue made me twitch.

"Come on, it's just a card. It won't bite." She wiggled the card.

"What do I even say?"

"Ask him a question. Ask him about the investigation. Guys like to feel needed and smart." She jabbed the card toward me again.

"I do want to apologize to him. I can't stop feeling like I was really rude." I plucked the card from her fingers, running my thumb over his name. "I feel silly, being so nervous about this."

Kylie gave me an eyeroll. "Don't be so dramatic. I seriously doubt you were rude. It's practically impossible for you. Even when you *need* to be rude, you can't. What you are is super sensitive. And also sexy as hell, and he knows it. If he doesn't, he's stupid and not worth your time. Harness your inner goddess and give the man a call. If he's even remotely interested, he'll take that phone call as an invitation."

I drew in a deep breath and blew it out, forcibly relaxing my shoulders. I could do this. It was a simple phone call.

"Sit with me while I do this?" I asked Kylie.

She grinned and passed me my cell.

Chapter 4

Mike

I couldn't stop the grin that spread across my face as I hung up the phone.

"What's that look for at 7:30 in the morning? Who was on the phone?" Thoren asked, passing me a fresh cup of coffee.

Captain Mac Collins had called and asked me to stop by before the start of my shift at the PD, which was at the end of his twenty-four-hour shift. So I was waiting on him in the firehouse's day room when Leah called.

"That was the sexy yoga instructor I told you about last night," I said, feeling smug. She'd called with an innocent question, but I'd turned it into an opportunity to stop by for a visit later. Buoyed with the knowledge that I'd see her soon, I couldn't wipe the smile off my face.

"You look like the cat who got the canary," Big Mo said, walking into the room and going to refill his water bottle from the spout on the fridge. "I take it you've got plans on seeing your lady later?"

"As a matter of fact, I do."

"Better get in the gym and get those muscles all pumped up before you go," he teased.

"Shut up, smartass," I muttered, but couldn't help enjoying the ribbing he gave. Nothing could dampen this morning.

"Oh good, you made it." Captain Collins's deep voice interrupted the teasing. "Come on back to my office."

I followed him down the hall of their brand-new station. Our town had grown over the years, necessitating this new facility. The stationed buzzed with quiet efficiency but didn't have an overbearing feel like the main public safety headquarters downtown. Probably because this station was free from administrative bullshit. But none of that meant as much as the closeness I noticed the crew shared. They were like a family. I envied them that.

"Have a seat," Captain Collins offered as we entered his office. "I wanted to let you know that there is a new position coming soon. With the recent uptick in structure fires, and our community's growing population, Administration has finally agreed that the fire investigator/inspection team needs to become a full-time position."

Anticipation shot through me. I envied the close relationships between the guys here, and there was a possibility to become one of them?

"That's good news, sir. And I agree, it's definitely a needed position. My captain gives me shit all the time about working a fire case instead of working my patrol route. It can be difficult to manage."

He nodded once and studied me with his hard gaze. I was not a small person and didn't get intimidated often, but there was something about Captain Collins that made a guy question his manhood. I fought the urge to squirm in my seat under his scrutiny.

"I know, that's the other part of it. Off the record, the police chief has been bitching, and we're sick of it. Also off the record, if you are remotely interested, I want you for the job." He paused, his quiet words ringing loud and clear in my head. "The other guy just doesn't get the job done. I think he spends half his time parked in front of the car wash. I know I caught him loafing one day and had words with the chief. Fact is, you've closed ninety percent of the cases. In my mind, you're a shoo-in for the job. But you think about it, because I know your family is law enforcement, and this would fall under the firehouse. It would also mean you'd have to go back to the academy and get your fire certification."

Going through rookie school wouldn't be that big of a deal. But he'd hit upon the one thing that might hold me back. My family would never understand me choosing the fire department over the police department. The Harrisons had been in the police department for four generations.

Still, the idea called to me. And I'd never been one to follow the expectations of my family.

"Thank you for your confidence in me, sir."

"Keep a watch. They should be posting the position by the end of the week. You'll have to put in for it, but you've got the skills and the proven track record. And I'll go to bat for you."

Fighting off the uncomfortable emotion those words elicited, I stood to shake his hand. "Thank you again, sir. I'll let you know if I apply."

I left the station feeling a strange combination of elated, hesitant, and excited. On the one hand, my family would probably disown me if I told them I wanted to move into the fire service. On the other, it was still doing investigative work, so maybe they'd understand. But now, it was time to set that opportunity out of my mind because I was on my way to meet with my yoga instructor, and hopefully convince her to have dinner with me.

Chapter 5

Leah

I paced the front lobby, waiting for Officer Harrison. This, of course, was ridiculous. We hadn't set a time that he'd show up when we talked on the phone, and I'd hung up only a couple minutes ago. He just said he'd stop by. I really should've confirmed a time with him so I wouldn't have to spend my day on pins and needles waiting. In my defense, it was Kylie's fault that I'd acted on the spur of the moment and called him before normal business hours.

"Stop pacing—you're being ridiculous," she muttered from the check-in counter.

I wrung my hands as I reached the edge of the room and then doubled back. "I can't help it. I'm nervous."

"What's to be nervous about?"

I rolled my eyes. "That's easy for you to say. I'd love to be so nonchalant. You're beautiful, with perfect hair and skin. You're outgoing. You've never met a man that didn't fall in love with you at first sight." I stopped to really look at her. She had no idea what a catch she was. "You've got more charisma in your pinkie finger than I do in my entire body."

Kylie looked up at my words and cocked her head to the side. "This is strangely fascinating. I've never seen you act this way. Not even when we were in college. This small town has had some weird effect on your dating mojo. It definitely has on mine," she finished on a mutter.

She and I had started a successful yoga program together on campus but had lost our close connection after graduation. On a road trip to visit my parents last year, my car had broken down and I'd fallen in love with this quaint little town while I'd waited on repairs. So when I was ready to set up my new studio, doing it with my business bestie in this place felt right.

Kylie turned to study me. "Where is your calm-cool-chill, Leah?"

We'd installed a small bell to alert us when the front door opened, since we couldn't actually see the entryway from the sign-in desk. The bell jingled and my heart raced in response, totally not calm or cool.

I held my breath, facing the doorway, awkwardly shifting my hand from the top of the desk to my side and back again. Neither position felt natural, so I was caught in a weird stance when Officer Harrison stepped into the room.

"Hello, Officer Hottie." Kylie's voice was low enough that he probably couldn't hear her. Probably. God, she was going to embarrass me, I just knew it.

He smiled at Kylie from the doorway, before locking eyes with me.

My knees went weak.

His uniform was crisp and sharp. Not a speck of dust, not a wrinkle in sight. His hair close-cropped, and face sporting a clean shave. The wide utility belt at his waist held a variety of scary looking police-y items and creaked with every step he took toward us.

"Hello again." His deep voice echoed his smile and sent a wave of shivers down my spine. I could imagine that voice soft in my ear, demanding I do as he pleased.

And yet, even as I stood paralyzed at the sight of him, I felt more than saw Kylie shift and sidle around the counter. As she drew into my periphery, I recognized her saucy walk for what it was, and my blood boiled with jealousy. She was sex on legs, and I was...not. If we'd been colors, hers would be a dark seductive red, and mine would be a pale yellow.

"Welcome to Blue Lotus. I'm Kylie." Why was her voice so sultry and raspy? Was my best friend seriously hitting on this man when I'd confessed to being interested in him?

I watched in horror as he reached out and took her offered hand.

"It's nice to meet you, Kylie."

I expected a lingering hand hold, a long gaze into her eyes, the exploration of Kylie's perfect face. That's what normally happened when she bewitched a guy. I'd seen it happen too many times. But surprisingly, he dropped her hand and turned to me. The change in his gaze was subtle, but I caught it. All my nerve endings lit up as he took a step closer to me.

"I'm glad you called, Leah." He flashed a grin, and God help me, he had a dimple. How a dimple survived on this badass man I had no idea. "Is there somewhere that we can talk?"

I squeaked a yes and led him out to the front porch, offering him a seat in one of the wide rockers. Perching on the chair next to his, I gripped my knees like an awkward teenager. I'd never made a move on a man before, and I was

out of my element. He exuded power, strength, authority–
the complete opposite of my usual type.

Swallowing my nerves, I met his gaze. "I wanted to apologize to you for being so dismissive yesterday, and it felt insincere to do so over the phone. I had something on my mind, and then you were there and then you were gone, but I thought about it...you...how rude I was all night, so I'm glad you came by."

I couldn't look at him after my word vomit, but the creak of his belt as he shifted drew my attention back to him. He leaned toward me, elbow braced on the chair arm.

"You wanna know a secret?" The glint in his eye and the way his mouth tipped at the corner in a not-quite smile were mesmerizing.

I'd barely nodded before that not-quite smile grew to a full grin, and that dimple popped out. "I was coming by here today anyway."

I frowned. "Was there a problem with your inspection?"

"No, but I would've found some excuse."

I wanted to believe that there was some alternative reason and hoped that reason might be that he was equally interested in me. The scrape of the chair as he shifted closer skittered across my frazzled nerves. I was certain he could hear my heart pounding, could feel the nervous energy I had to be radiating. He leaned toward me, eyes twinkling. His tongue peaked out to wet his lips and I stopped breathing.

"And then, I would've found a way to work that excuse into a reason to ask you out for dinner."

He reached out, his hand landing on the arm of my chair, so close to touching me I could almost feel it. "So now that we don't need any more preliminary excuses, will you have dinner with me tonight?"

The eye twinkle shifted to seductive heat. If I read his gaze right, he wanted to devour me. There was no way I'd ever survive a man like him, but I was willing to give it a try.

"Yes, I'll have you for dinner."

The dimple was back, along with the grin. He reached up to brush a tendril of hair off my shoulder with the barest graze of his fingertip, leaving a trail of fire in its wake.

Then I realized what I'd said.

"Oh my god! I meant—Yes. I mean, I'd like to have dinner *with* you."

He stood and braced his hands on the arms of my chair. Leaning in, he brushed his lips across my cheekbone. "I liked your first answer better. Seven o'clock work for you?"

Words failed me. Lost in a riot of hormones, I didn't trust myself to speak anyway. Who knew what would come out of my traitorous mouth? So I simply nodded. He shifted the barest amount, softly inhaling at that sensitive spot on my neck, just below my ear, where I usually rubbed my favorite oils.

"I can't wait," he whispered.

He lingered a second longer, then pushed off my chair and backed away. "Text me your address." At the sidewalk he looked back, leaving me with a smile. "See you tonight."

After a full five minutes of recovery, I managed to make my way back into the studio where Kylie met me in the hall, just beyond the door.

"Girl! You didn't tell me he was so hot!" Her exuberance over the hotness of my date left a sourness in my mouth.

"You didn't have to go all sex-kitten on him," I grumped.

"Yes, I did. I had to test and see if his eye was easily turned. He passed of course. That man only had eyes for you."

"And you couldn't do that in another way?" Kylie sometimes had the weirdest methods of showing her love.

"Probably, but I also needed to get you out of your head. You should've seen how you bristled." She bounced on her toes excitedly. "And girl. You got so mad, I could almost see the steam coming out of your ears. But enough about that. What happened outside? Tell me everything!"

As usual, Kylie had a way of shifting my focus. "He asked me out. He's taking me to dinner tonight." For some reason, I didn't want to share about the brush of his lips that I could still feel. "Will you cover my class for me?"

"Absolutely. And in between classes, we are glamming you up and raiding my closet."

"I don't know about that." Kylie had a closet full of clothes, and every outfit fell solidly in the sexy or skimpy category.

"I've got the perfect dress for you. It's been hanging in my closet begging for opportunity, never been worn. And alas," she sighed dramatically, "I'm on a dating hiatus. So, you have to wear it."

Chapter 6

Mike

I'd stalled as long as I could, but finally I just said to hell with it because I couldn't wait to see Leah. That's how I found myself pulling up at the curb in front of her place a quarter of an hour early. Hell, just thinking her name did weird things to my belly and had my heart all fluttery. What a douche. Had I really lost all semblance of badass cool?

I checked my goofiness as I stepped out of the car and scanned the street. The low hum of a distant lawnmower serenaded the early evening in her quaint neighborhood. This part of town was well established. Mostly older homes with trimmed yards and short picket fences lined a curving street just a few blocks from her studio. Her neighborhood felt alive with people out enjoying the evening, walking dogs, and visiting with neighbors.

Hanging baskets overflowing with green plants covered the full front porch of her bungalow. A well-tended flowerbed followed her front walk from the mailbox to the wide porch steps. The neighborhood was safe. We didn't run many, if any, police calls in the area. The whole place felt homey. It was a far cry from my barely-furnished apartment in a neighborhood where residents ignored each other. She'd settled into her place, made it her own, and was thriving. I'd been floundering around, not making my mark, even in my own living space.

I knocked on her door and stepped back, nervously adjusting the lapel of my sport coat and trying hard not to squeeze the bouquet of flowers I'd picked up. It was unusual for me to be nervous about a date, but I wanted to make a good impression. I wanted her to like me because I sure as hell liked her. I'd spent the whole day thinking about her, obsessed by the scent of her.

The hairs on the back of my neck prickled. Was I being watched? I glanced over my shoulder, trying to find the source.

The clip of heels sounded from inside the house, and then the door swung open. And my breath just stopped.

She stood before me in a long satiny red dress. Thin, fragile-looking straps crossed her shoulders, and I wondered what it would take to snap them.

"Hi." She smiled and I was fully caught in her trap as that voice washed over me.

Her hair was styled in a half-up, half-down mass of waves, exposing the curve of her neck. I drank in the sight of her, aching to discover if her skin was as soft as it looked.

"Are those for me?" She tilted her head toward the forgotten bouquet in my hand. Unable to form words, I held them out to her. Her eyes lit with amusement as she rescued the bundle from my grip, burying her nose in the colorful mix. "These are lovely, Mike, thank you. Let me drop these in water and grab my bag and I'm ready to go." She swung the door wider, inviting me inside, and turned away.

I took one step inside and froze, arrested by the sight of

her walking away. The dress draped her body as she moved, just tight enough to showcase the swell of her breasts, the curve of her ass. Those fragile straps ended around her shoulder blades, leaving the fabric to drape lower, exposing the smooth expanse of her back. With every step she took, the dress shifted in a sexy highlight of her toned body.

She filled a funky-looking pottery vase with water and dropped the flowers in. After grabbing her bag, she made her way back to me, a toned leg peeping out from the slit in the dress. I couldn't drag my eyes away from her.

Stopping in front of me, she gripped the bag in front of her, breaking the spell I was under.

"Damn, Leah. That dress..." I licked my lips as my words failed me.

Jesus, man, get a grip. I was normally a classier asshole than this.

But color was high on her cheeks, and she was breathing just as quickly as I was.

"Plans just changed," I declared.

Her face fell. "What? Why?"

I gave into temptation, and touched a tendril of hair, mesmerized with the way it curled around my finger. "Because I'd picked a place where we could just talk and spend time together. And now, I'm thinking I need to take you somewhere that I can get you on a dance floor and into my arms."

Her lush lips parted as she inhaled, and then she beamed at me. "Do you like it?"

I was a goner. Just...boom. Gone for her. As if my heart just leapt right out of my chest and plopped itself on the floor at her feet. In that moment, with that one smile, I knew I'd do everything in my power to earn another.

"Definitely."

I held the door as she locked up, and her hand as we hit the stairs, savoring the electric pulse the connection sent up my arm.

"Do you mind if we make a quick stop before we go to dinner?" she asked.

"Not at all. What'd you have in mind?"

She gestured across the street. "I need to check on my neighbor, Francis. She's elderly and lives alone so I check on her nearly every day. I was in a rush earlier and didn't get to stop by." Just like I'd thought, these people took care of each other.

I motioned for her to lead the way, tucking her hand in the crook of my arm as we crossed the street. At the sidewalk she called, "Hey, Mrs. Francis."

I looked up to see a spry elderly woman leaning on a porch rail, watching us like a hawk. "I was wondering if you were going to stop by this fine evening."

Leah chuckled as we climbed the few steps. "Yes, ma'am. I was just running late. Kylie went a little overboard today." She dropped my arm as we reached the top and embraced the elderly woman.

Beneath a cloud of soft white curls, the woman eyeballed me head to toe. "And who is this handsome fella you've brought me? He looks awfully familiar," she said with a twinkle in her eye.

"This is my friend Mike. Mike, this is Mrs. Francis O'Malley. We were just going to dinner."

"I bet that's not all you're doing," the old lady mumbled, turning to guide us to a row of rocking chairs. "Come sit a spell."

"Oh, we can't stay long. I just wanted to stop by on our

way out." Leah leaned her back against the porch rail, her pose casual, but I got the impression that she was watching every movement Mrs. O'Malley made.

Mrs. O'Malley settled into her rocking chair and picked up a mug, taking a long pull and keeping one eye aimed at me. With a smack of her lips, she pointed at me with the mug. "I know where I know you. It took me a minute, because you're wearing clothes, but I'm almost positive I recognize that jawline. If you were shirtless, I'd have no doubt." She nodded at her own statement. "You were in the public safety calendar, weren't you, young man?"

Heat crept up from the collar of my dress shirt, and Leah went rigid beside me. Normally I could turn on the charm when someone mentioned the calendar. But under her scrutiny, I felt like I might as well have been naked right there on her front porch. "Yes, ma'am. I was in this year's calendar."

"Mrs. O'Malley, please don't make my date uncomfortable," Leah chided softly.

"Oh, pshaw. There's no shame in me appreciating all that hard work he does at the gym." She winked at Leah. "You're in for a fun evening if things go your way, dear."

Leah turned bright red but still managed to level a stern look while I stood by and tried not to choke. "Mrs. O," she admonished, "there's no tea in that mug, is there?"

The older woman scoffed. "Now why would I mess up a perfectly good bourbon by putting tea in it?"

"You've got a point there." I pressed my lips together, trying not to laugh.

"You two go enjoy a lovely evening." The older woman shooed us with her mug. "I'm gonna sit right here until Eunice makes her nightly stroll so I can let her know I got to meet Mr. July." Her eyes scanned my frame, lingering on my torso before dipping lower. "Oh, I have that calendar memorized, sugar."

I barely stopped the shudder before Leah saved the day. "Behave, Francis. Quit making my date awkward." She leaned to kiss the older woman on the cheek, distracting me with her backless dress again.

I ushered her across the street and to my car.

"Thanks for stopping by Francis's with me," Leah said as we turned off her road.

I nodded through a haze of lust. I'd been so distracted by the dress, I'd missed her toned legs. But the moment she'd slid in my car, my focus had shifted and now I was fighting a hard-on, again, while trying to deliver us to dinner safely.

"Sure, no problem. She seems like a character." It took some work to make my tone sound normal.

"She's harmless, mostly." Leah chuckled. "She generally knows the best gossip, and has an unhealthy obsession with abs." Her voice grew quiet, pensive. "But other times, she's a lonely widow that needs someone to look in on her."

I cut my gaze to her at a stop sign. "And you do that? Keep tabs on her and make sure she's okay?"

Leah nodded, a small smile tugging at the corner of her mouth. "It can be a challenge to keep her out of trouble, especially on penny poker night. Francis and Eunice tend to argue, hotly, and have this weird competition over who has the best piece of gossip. But yes. I check in with her every day."

The conversation shifted as we headed downtown, then parked and walked to the restaurant. Live music set the mood inside, and I spotted a pianist playing a gleaming baby grand in the corner. Leah paused for a moment to listen.

As the hostess led us to a table, I followed Leah with a

hand at the small of her back, making sure every joker in the room knew she was mine.

Once we'd ordered, I said, "So, tell me, why yoga?"

She relaxed back into her chair and picked up her wine, savoring a sip before answering. "I took some classes in college. That's actually where I met Kylie. We got our yoga certifications together, then started our own program. I love everything about it. There's something powerful in harnessing the body, and something spiritual in releasing the emotions we hold in. Yoga allows you to focus on the now."

"How'd you end up here? And why haven't we ever met? This town isn't that big. How have I missed you all this time?" I was inclined to be up front with her and not try to hide my feelings. She'd probably see right through me anyway.

"My folks retired nearby, and I ended up here to start my own studio with Kylie last year, mainly because my grandma passed away and left me her house. And we've probably not met because I tend to keep to myself." She fiddled with her wineglass. "What about you? Why law enforcement?"

I stared into her beautiful eyes and answered honestly. "Because it's my family legacy. Dad, brother, grandad, all cops."

"You don't seem thrilled when you say that."

How'd she know that? "Maybe I'm not. Lately it feels like something is missing."

"Is there something else you'd rather do?"

I didn't answer because that uncomfortable feeling I'd had when I'd stood on her doorstep came back. She was just as settled in her career as she was her house. The contrast between our situations pricked a nerve. Rattled by the direction of our conversation, and how exposed it made me feel, I steered us to safer topics.

We chatted for a while longer, until I'd had all I could take. No one else seemed to take note of the empty dance floor, but it called to me. More than ready to have her in my arms, I stood and offered my hand.

She smiled shyly but placed her hand in mine and allowed me to lead her to the dance floor. I spun her around and finally–finally–she was in my arms.

"We're the only ones out here," she murmured, gazing into my eyes. I slipped my hand across her lower back, taking advantage of the low-cut dress by brushing my thumb across her heated skin.

"I don't care. I want the world to see you in my arms." I pulled her closer.

"You look at me as if…"

I watched her closely, taking in every feature. "As if what?" I prompted, wanting to know how she saw me.

"As if you really like me," she said softly, almost like she didn't believe it.

Her words drew a smile from me. "I do."

"Why?"

"For starters, you're the most beautiful woman I've ever laid eyes on. But it goes beyond that. You're fascinating to me. The way you view the world differently than I do. You check on your neighbor just because you're nice, and you literally stopped to smell the flowers at the shop next door. You took a moment to really listen to the piano player when we came in here. You live in the moment and seem to appreciate every aspect of life."

She blushed the tiniest bit, but her gaze never left mine.

"It's in the way you look at me. Like you are right now. Like there is no expectation, except…maybe the desire to know me better." I paused. Despite the uncomfortable awareness the evening had brought, all of it dimmed in comparison to how much I liked this woman. How drawn I was to her. "I need to kiss you, Leah."

She let out a breath, and pressed against my chest, whispering, "So kiss me."

Chapter 7

Leah

I leaned into Mike, rising on my toes, wanting nothing more than to taste his lips. His dark gaze held mine as he lowered his head. My eyelids fluttered closed as his mouth caressed mine in a gentle exploration. My heart expanded under his gentle touch.

He'd been chivalrous and attentive all evening, and oh-so-sweet when he'd offered me flowers. Timid, almost. As if he didn't want to take anything for granted. Just like this kiss, a soft meeting of our lips, a hesitant expectation. It all changed as he angled his head, his tongue tracing across my lips. I opened to him, seeking more of him, inviting him. His arms tightened around me as I lost myself in his kiss. We were alone on the dance floor in the middle of a crowded restaurant, the center of attention, and I didn't care one bit. By the time he stopped kissing me, we were both breathing heavy, and I was ready to throw my heart at his feet, or at least invite him back to my place.

He pulled away, resting his forehead on mine. He began a gentle sway, leading my body in a way that told me if I did invite him in, we'd spend the evening making love.

"Best date in the history of ever," I whispered with a smile.

"And it's not over yet." He returned my smile before kissing my nose. "Let's get out of here."

In response, I stepped out of his arms, twining my fingers with his, leading him from the dance floor to collect our things.

A familiar face caught my eye as we passed a booth, and I paused, my heart tripping now for a different reason. "Hi, Karen. Hello, Mr. Lindell."

I didn't miss the flash of surprise and hesitation from Karen as Mr. Lindell turned his head to greet me.

"Hello, Leah. What a surprise to see you here. How are things at your little studio?"

Every time I spoke with Mr. Lindell, he made me feel as if he looked down on me and my business. As if him being our landlord gave him some superiority over us. He was a pretentious jerk, and we just had to suck it up and deal.

"And Michael!" he continued. "This is a nice surprise. How are you, son? It's so good to see you."

I froze, shocked, as Mr. Lindell stood and reached out. Mike curled around me to shake his hand.

"Hi, Richard, Karen. How are you?" he said easily.

It was obvious they knew each other, were very familiar. I shouldn't have expected any less in this small town, but still...it was uncomfortable to stand in front of them while I harbored suspicions.

"You know each other?" Karen finally spoke, her voice as stilted and awkward as I felt. "You're here together?"

Mike pulled me closer, his hand sliding across my lower back before settling at my waist where he gave a small squeeze. "We are." He sounded so happy, and that settled some of the trepidation I felt seeing Karen with the man I suspected was abusing her.

"How are your parents?" Mr. Lindell addressed Mike, launching into conversation, dismissing Karen and I in the process. I took the opportunity to glance at her.

"How are you?" I asked, my words holding a weight beyond politeness. I hoped she understood what I was really asking.

"I'm well. This afternoon's class was really great. I enjoyed the restorative session."

What she didn't know was that I'd planned that whole session hoping she would be in class. I didn't want to further stress her body. She was still moving tenderly.

"I'm so glad you enjoyed it."

Mike wrapped up his conversation with a firm "it was great to see you." With a final nod toward the couple, he tugged me out of the restaurant.

Twinkle lights were strung in the trees that lined the sidewalk, lending the evening a romantic glow as we strolled the downtown streets. But the ambiance of the evening had been tilted sideways for me, and I was no longer feeling the glow of earlier.

I was upset at the thought of what Karen faced at home, and I didn't know how to help. If I tried to force the situation, I could very well make things worse for her. I'd learned that lesson once before. But she clearly wouldn't admit that any abuse was going on.

"Do you want to talk about what just happened back there?" Mike asked.

"What do you mean?" I asked, not wanting to divulge my suspicions without any proof. It was obvious that Mike was fond of the couple.

"Something made you tense, uncomfortable. What was it?"

I tried to shake off my worry and divert his questioning by slipping my hand into his and smiling up at him.

"It's nothing. Something about them remind me of another couple I once knew." I leaned in so that our arms touched from shoulder to wrist as we walked. "That dance was lovely, thank you. Do you like to dance often?"

The look in his eye and answering smile left me breathless. "Only with pretty ladies in red dresses," he said, squeezing my hand.

It was late by the time we got to my house and Mike walked me to the door, but I didn't want the evening to be over. I turned to him, scrambling for any excuse to get him to stay.

He stepped close, backing me up to the porch wall, and cupped my face.

"I don't want this night to be over, Leah." His words were an echo of my own desire.

I slid my hand up the wide expanse of his chest, marveling at the ridges underneath his shirt. Something about him made me feel safe. Like the world could burn down around me and he would shield me from it.

"Me neither," I responded.

I caught his darkened gaze just before his mouth lowered to mine. Our lips met in a kiss that quickly had us both breathing heavily, and ended with me pressed against the wall, my free leg hooked over his hip, and his large hand gripping my thigh as our bodies ground together. Too many layers of fabric couldn't hide the hard ridge that pressed against my center, and I was there for it. I wanted him inside my house, then inside me.

He ripped himself away with a rasped "fuck." He lifted

a hand and brushed a strand of hair from my forehead, trailing his fingertips across my cheek before gliding the soft pad of his thumb across my lip. "You are so beautiful. And when you kiss me like that, baby, it makes me want to take you inside and get you out of that dress."

I liked the sound of that. "How would you do it?" My words were whispered and heated and all I could think was that I'd let this man do anything he wanted to me.

He leaned forward, tucking his head and raining kisses down my neck. I tilted my head to allow him better access.

"I'd start with this tiny little strap. I'd slip it off this sexy shoulder." With the tip of his finger, he slid a strap off, his lips following the path, creating a trail of heat that left me writhing and my panties wet. He pressed his hips into mine, letting me feel the effect this was having on him as well. My hands drifted to his belt to pull him closer.

"Then I would peel it off of you, and let it drop to the floor." He traced the curve of my shoulder with a fingertip, tracing the exposed skin along the edge of the fabric strap of my dress, leaving a trail of goosebumps behind every place his warm skin touched mine. A shiver cascaded down my spine. I pictured us wrapped in each other's arms, our naked bodies sliding skin on skin, and I ached.

Car lights flashed over us as a neighbor turned down the street and passed my house, making us both pause and seem to realize that we were on my porch. I slumped back against the wall, meeting his hot gaze.

For a long moment we stood, each trying to catch our breath, clearly on the same page and wanting more. I might have regrets in the morning, but right now, all I wanted was more of him.

Finally, he brushed the back of a finger across the apple of my cheek. "No, I don't want this night to end." His finger slipped under my chin, lifting it to meet his kiss. Against my lips he whispered, "But...I want to do this right with you."

I closed my eyes, disappointed, but appreciative. And scared to admit the truth. "This thing between us feels big, doesn't it?"

He pulled me tighter into his embrace, resting his head against mine. His chest rose on a long inhale. "Yeah, gorgeous. It does."

I turned to rest my cheek on his chest, savoring the closeness. I didn't know where we were headed, but at least we were on the same page.

Chapter 8

Leah

Mike had been all gentlemanly after our date and left me at the front door. And I'd spent most of the night awake and most of the morning distracted–even failing to be nosy about Karen's situation when she'd arrived for class. For the most part we'd ignored our previous encounter and acted like nothing was wrong.

That didn't stop my lingering concerns about her. She was quiet and introspective in class, and I really wanted to talk to her about it. But since I didn't know how to handle the situation, and certainly didn't want to make her uncomfortable, I swallowed my apprehension and bit my tongue.

I cleaned and closed the practice room and stepped into the hall. Voices carried from the lobby, and while a lilting feminine laugh wasn't unusual to hear in the studio, the deep familiar male voice that responded was, and it grabbed my attention and drew me forward. I'd been hearing that voice in my dreams.

I rounded the corner to find Karen talking with Mike,

her demeanor completely changed. She was smiling and friendly, almost flirty.

"Well, it was good to see you, Michael. Tell your mom I said hi."

He gifted her one of those gorgeous smiles. "I will. I'm sure she'll want you and Richard to come over for cocktails or something. She lives for that."

"That'd be wonderful. I'll give her a call."

I watched Karen leave, her movements controlled but graceful. She hid her discomfort well. Too well. As if she was practiced in masking pain.

"You okay?"

Mike's voice broke my train of thought, and I turned to find him watching me.

"Sorry." I offered an apologetic smile, burying my concerns. "Just distracted."

His expression shifted as he studied my face. I'd never had anyone look so closely at me and flushed under the attention. He seemed to see inside my soul.

"Everything okay?" he repeated.

Part of me wanted to confide in him, trust him to help me determine what—if anything—I could do next. But Karen's situation wasn't my story to tell. And he obviously knew her, so I couldn't divulge her secrets.

In the end, I simply nodded and offered him a smile. "Yes, just have a lot on my mind, I guess. What brings you by?" I hoped it was because he wanted to see me.

"I just wanted to drop off a copy of your report," he said, deflating my hope as he lifted the envelope in his hand. Then he leaned toward me with a suggestive grin playing on his lips, and hope returned. "And I wanted to see you."

My heart fluttered as I drank in the sight of him. I'd lain awake all night thinking about how differently I'd imagined the evening ending, and then appreciative that he'd wanted to take things slowly. By the time morning had rolled around I was a mess of hormones, and all I could think of was what if he'd stayed.

His mouth was right there. All it would take would be the slightest shift...we needed to get out of the middle of the studio before I embarrassed myself by attacking him. I wanted to see if my memory of those kisses we'd shared was accurate, but I didn't want an audience. I ushered him out of the hallway and back towards the office area.

"I'm glad you stopped by," I said, all business as I led us through the studio and pushed through the door to the small office.

He stepped into the space and immediately the room felt smaller. I leaned on the edge of the desk. Mike stepped closer, my gaze immediately darting to his lips. His delicious, talented lips.

"Why'd you bring me back here, Leah?" His eyes burned, drifting down to my lips then back up. He tossed the envelope onto the desk beside me.

I hadn't wanted a man like this in a long time. But Mike was so sensual, just being near him made all my nerve endings flare. I ran a hand over my hair to get refocused and tried to get my hormones under control.

"I don't like talking business out front where my clients can eavesdrop. If it's not membership related, we tend to hold our discussions here in private."

When I looked at him again, he was a step closer, in my space. All it would take was a slight movement on my part and our bodies would touch.

His brows rose, and he looked at me curiously. "Not the answer I was expecting."

His full lips had me entranced. I licked mine,

wondering what he would think if I just leaned forward and tasted him. "What were you expecting?"

His eyes sharpened on me and he stepped closer, slipping a hand to my waist. "I don't know, but with the way you keep looking at my mouth...I think..." With slow movements and his gaze locked on mine, he closed the distance between us. My breath caught as our chests brushed.

His lips were pillow soft as they met mine.

Desire flooded me. This kiss was even better than the ones after our date last night.

He pulled away slightly and whispered, "I was hoping this might be why you wanted privacy."

I smiled and grabbed his shirt, yanking him back to me. "Well, now that you mention it..."

This kiss was deeper, and he pulled me into his body. For long drugging moments, he explored my mouth. By the time he pulled away, we were both panting, and I was left wanting more. Again.

He rested his forehead against mine again. That was quickly becoming one of my favorite things. "I've been wanting to do that since the moment I woke up." His voice was low and rough and hit me square in the heart. "But," he said as he moved back and grabbed the envelope he'd brought with him, "I do have the inspection report for you and also a question."

I took the envelope. "What's the question?" I prompted.

He pulled me back into his arms. "Have dinner with me again?"

* * *

"Hi." I smiled as soon as I opened my door to Mike. He'd insisted on picking me up, even though I thought it was ridiculous for him to come get me, just to return to his apartment.

But he'd declared, "It's a date, just humor me." So I let him do his thing. Who was I to argue if the guy wanted to be sweet and chivalrous? And he was, ushering me to the car with a hand at my back, opening doors for me. The way he treated me made me feel like a million bucks.

"Smells good in here," I said as he let us into his apartment. He deposited the bottle of wine I'd brought in the fridge, wiping his palms on his jeans before turning to slip a dish out of the oven. "Make yourself at home," he called over his shoulder.

I took my time surveying his apartment. He had some brand-new throw pillows on the couch, still bearing the tags. "I see you made a HomeGoods run. Want me to remove these tags? Or are you still deciding on them?"

I glanced at him after a beat of silence. He looked flustered, muttering under his breath as he rummaged through a drawer. I went to him and crowded his space, slipping my arms around his waist. I had a sneaking suspicion that he'd made a special throw-pillow run just for my benefit. I was charmed, seeing him so nervous.

"Did you buy throw pillows to impress me?"

"You weren't supposed to find out, but I got behind making dinner and forgot to remove the tags."

"You're too sweet." I pressed a kiss to his cheek and felt the warmth of his hands slip around my waist. Drawing back, I bit my lip, unsure what I could say that would ease his nerves. His hot gaze focused on my lips.

"When you do that, it makes me want to bite that lip." His low, sexy voice sent a thrill through me.

Instant panty combustion. If I'd had any doubt before about how he felt, and what he wanted, the desire on

Mike's face cleared it right up. This cozy dinner at his apartment was headed straight to the bedroom, and I was so on board with that idea. I drank in the way his t-shirt molded over his strong chest, the way his jeans cupped his body. I immediately wanted to strip them off and explore the body underneath, first with my eyes, then my hands and lips.

He closed the distance between us, his heated gaze roaming my face before locking on my mouth. My body thrummed with awareness. He was so big, and desire radiated off him.

I wanted this man more than I'd ever wanted anyone. Beyond his obvious good looks, there was something elemental in the connection we had.

I slipped my fingers into the waistband of his jeans, tugging him closer. "Kiss me, Mike."

He needed no further invitation, crushing his body to mine, lifting me so that I was pressed against his hard chest. My whole body sighed because this felt so right.

I shifted, wrapping my legs around his waist, moaning at the feel of his body between my legs.

He backed me to the counter, grinding into me.

"Fuck, Leah," he growled.

"Yes, let's do that," I whispered against his lips.

He drew back, his questioning eyes searching mine. From my position on the counter, I was just enough taller than him that I felt powerful, in control. And the fire in his gaze made me feel wanted.

Unable to resist, I leaned forward and licked that delicious looking lower lip, before settling my mouth over his again. We were a blazing inferno, and each stroke of his tongue against mine fanned the flames higher.

I pulled away to catch my breath, and he shifted that

glorious mouth, nipping his way across my jaw, scraping his teeth across the sensitive lobe of my ear.

"Dinner first or after?" I gasped against the onslaught of what his mouth was doing to me.

He reached over and turned the oven off, then scooped me off the counter and carried me out of the kitchen.

Slipping my hands under his shirt, my fingertips grazing his warm skin, I struggled to get closer and get him naked at the same time. I needed to feel his body pressed to mine, skin on skin. My back hit the couch, and he raised up, stripped our clothes off, and then he was on me, cupping my jaw as his tongue thrust into my mouth. Consuming me, lighting me on fire with his drugging kisses. His hands slid from my jaw to my neck, his mouth following the path his hands made.

He took his time kissing down my body, exploring every inch of me. Devouring me. Caressing me from shoulder to waist, where he gripped and pulled my hips to his.

I ran my hands down his rippled chest, luxuriating in the feel of him. His low groan at my touch sent a thrill through me.

He kissed my breasts, licking and sucking, his teeth barely grazing a nipple. I gasped, throwing my head back. My core clenched hard.

Squirming beneath him, my body moving with the desire to know more, to feel more, I drove my hands into his hair and dragged him back to my mouth. He broke the kiss with a curse and sat up, leaning back on his heels. He was glorious as he looked down at me, face dark with desire, his big chest heaving. He reached down and adjusted himself. The sight of him gripping his length, barely holding on, was hot as hell.

"Fuck, look at you. Writhing, needy. Are you wet for

me, baby?" His deep voice rang with approval. His palm landed on the valley between my breasts, then slid down in a move that was both adoring and claiming. I wanted him to make me his. I wanted to give him every ounce of pleasure. The look on his face demanded it.

Moving lower, brushing over my needy clit, he slid a finger through my folds.

"Fuck yeah, so wet." He bit his lip, watching his finger glide up and down.

My God, I was going to come just from watching him.

"I need to taste you," he growled, his big hands sliding up the outside of my thighs, gripping there and pulling one up over his shoulder. And then his mouth was on me, teasing, sucking, driving me insane. He devoured me like a starved man.

"More," I cried, squirming beneath him. I dove my fingers into his hair, gripping him as my pleasure built.

He slipped a finger inside me, easing some of the need but driving me higher. Smoothly, he lifted my leg off his shoulder and folded it back on my body, so that I was spread wide open, waiting and needy for him. I took in the length of him, proud and ready for me, as he grabbed a foil package from the table behind the couch and positioned the condom to roll it on. I pulled his hands away and finished the job for him.

The strength of his desire was written all over his face as he lined himself up at my entrance. I gasped as he pushed inside, my body molding and stretching to take all of him.

"You feel so good." The words left me on a breath.

He braced a hand on the arm of the couch, watching me where we were joined, and then he began to move with a delicious roll of his hips.

"Fuck, Leah, I wanted to make this so good for you. But you feel so...I'm not gonna last."

I clawed my fingers down his back to his firm butt and squeezed. "I don't need it to last. I just need it fast and hard."

At my words, Mike set a rhythm that stole my breath, pounding into me with an intensity that left me crying out his name as an explosive orgasm shimmered. Then he rolled his hips in a magical way and I detonated. And nothing else mattered, except that I knew that I'd never get enough of being with him.

Chapter 9

Mike

"Tell me about your best day ever," Leah whispered against me, her fingers brushing the smattering of hair on my chest.

It'd been a week since we'd become an "us." A week of dinners and conversation, stories and laughter. A week of the most amazing sex of my life.

I'd woken to the sight of her doing some yoga poses that highlighted her flexible, strong body, and had joined her on the floor, which led to her showing me exactly how limber she could be. And that led to me bending her over the end of the bed and having my way with her. After a mind-blowing round of orgasms, we were snuggled back in my bed, legs tangled and her head on my chest as we caught our breath.

I trailed my fingers up and down her back and took a minute to think about her question. I could've gone with the truth, the day I met her, but I didn't think she'd go for that. I could've given her the standard "graduation from the police academy," but another memory tugged harder.

"When I was a junior in high school, I won the State

Championship in track." I hoped she didn't hear the hollowness that I felt. A brush of her fingertips grounded me.

"And why was it the best day?"

"Because that was the day I learned to stand on my own, to be proud of myself, to depend only on myself. That hard work and dedication was worth it."

"It wasn't the win?"

"Not really."

"I bet your parents were very proud of you."

"I'll never know."

Her head popped up and she met my eyes. "They weren't there?"

I smoothed my hand over her hair and down her back, pressing her back to my chest. I couldn't look her in the eye and tell this story. It was too shameful. She seemed to sense the undercurrent of emotion roiling through me and pulled my other hand up to twine our fingers. Just being connected with her grounded me again. I wasn't the forgotten one, the unimportant one. She was letting me know she was here, with me.

The vise around my chest loosened and the words tumbled out.

"I wasn't the athlete my brother was. We both played Little League baseball growing up and I spent most of my years playing in the next age bracket so that we could be on the same team and my mom wouldn't have to deal with the nightmare of logistics of two ball players at two different fields. He was so talented. Seriously, he was on multiple state championship teams and even went on to play ball at college."

I paused, running my fingers through her hair, fixating on the silky texture as it caressed my fingers. I took a resigned breath and continued. "But I eventually got tired of being the youngest and worst on the team, riding the bench with little to no playing time. So when I was in middle school, I started running track. Turns out, all those years of playing up had given me one advantage. I was willing to push harder than most, and I had a knack for track and field games.

"When I was a junior, all that hard work came to fruition at the state championship."

She shifted against me, tugging me so that I turned to face her. "Why weren't your parents at your meet to see you win?"

I tugged her hand up between us, playing with her fingers, still unable to look her in the eye. "They were at Robert's scrimmage game."

I traced her delicate nails, trimmed and natural. She surprised me by pulling our hands to her lips and gently kissing my hand. I glanced up to meet her gaze, to find hers glossy and swimming with emotion.

"I wish I'd been there. I'd have been so proud of you."

In a flash I imagined a yard full of tow-headed little kids running circles around this spectacular woman, her at the center of their game, like the center of their universe. She'd never let one of her kids feel less-than or unworthy.

I cleared my throat because I suddenly wanted those kids to be mine.

"Anyway, it's the worst day because my family wasn't there to celebrate with me. But it's the best day because I realized that I could win at something, and I was no longer in my brother's shadow."

She kissed me then, a melding of our mouths that had her pressing me onto my back and rising over me. When our bodies joined this time, it was with our eyes wide open and locked on each other. It was like she could see into my soul.

As she stretched and writhed above me, she led our still clasped hands across her body and then mine, and eventually guided them to the pillow above my head. With our hands clasped, our eyes locked and bodies one, I realized I was done for this woman. I was hers and she was mine.

Much later, I scooped her back to my chest and wound my arms around her. "Tell me about your best-worst day."

She was silent for a moment, and I let her have the space to think. I shifted my body, loving how she fit me so completely that my body cupped hers. I'd never enjoyed being the big spoon quite so much.

"Once upon a time, I had a friend, Ariel. I thought we were friends anyway. I knew she had a new stepdad at home, and she hadn't been happy since he'd moved in. She came to school one day with these bruises all over her. She'd begged me not to say anything, but I told the teacher, thinking that was the right thing to do. I was so proud of myself for standing up for her. The teacher pulled Ariel aside after math class, and I was certain that they'd take care of my friend. We were supposed to have the rest of our classes together that day, but Ariel never came back to class. She didn't come back for the rest of the week. And when she did, she had the remnant of a black eye and her arm was in a cast."

Her shudder rocked against me, and I tightened my arms around her. When she spoke again, her voice trembled.

"She knew I'd been the one to tell. She never spoke to me again, and they moved during the summer." Her voice caught. "I tried to help, and only made it worse."

My heart cracked at her obvious pain. I'd been through this on a domestic case early in my law enforcement career and had learned how to deal with feeling helpless when you knew someone was in need. I hugged her close and pressed a kiss to her cheek. "Don't cry, baby. You thought you were helping."

"How are you supposed to protect someone who is too scared to ask for help? Or do the right thing when you know it will get someone hurt?"

I sighed deeply, my chest rising against her back. "I've seen that on the job. It's heartbreaking to watch someone who feels like they can't get out of a domestic situation. You want to do all the right things, but that person, the victim, also has to be willing to take the step. What you can do in the meantime is offer support, find resources for them. Show them that someone cares and that what they are experiencing is not the way it has to be. That they deserve and are worthy of a better life."

She wiped her face with a corner of the sheet before twisting in my arms. The sight of her wet lashes nearly broke me. She opened her mouth as if to speak and hesitated.

"What is it?"

She swallowed thickly before whispering, "What if I have some suspicions that one of my yoga students is being harmed? Is there someone or somewhere that can help her here?"

"Female victim?"

At her nod, the cop in me stood at attention, wanting the name of the son-of-a-bitch not only because he was an abusive bastard, but because his abuse was also hurting my woman. But I knew that without just cause, I couldn't do a damn thing. Instead, I'd guide Leah as best I could to get her friend help.

"Yeah, baby. I'll get you a list of resources in the morning."

Her soft fingers brushed my face, and she leaned in to kiss me. "Thank you," she whispered against my lips. Then she kissed me again, shifting and pulling me over her. I did my best to make her forget her worries by worshipping every inch of her body.

Later that morning I followed Leah out to her screened-in back porch, a cozy space filled with plants and wicker furniture. In the yard, birds chirped happily from the trees, and her late-blooming flowers lent a warm, homey feel. It was a far cry from my apartment, making me realize how blank and empty my space was. Her place was comfortable. It felt right. I could see myself enjoying being here.

I grabbed her laptop and a notepad and jotted down a list of names and safe houses while Leah did her morning "flow," as she called it. She claimed that she'd been interrupted on her first attempt. I didn't give a damn what it was called, I just knew she wore the tiniest shorts and stretchy band-top that looked like they could be ripped off by the slightest tug of my pinky finger.

Watching Leah do her thing was mesmerizing. Her body stretched and bent in an amazing display of power and strength. She pressed herself into a handstand and then spread her legs wide.

"Now you're just taunting me," I growled from the large wicker round seat. Come to think of it, the chair was big enough for the two of us...

She chuckled. "Maybe."

After a series of backbends and stretches that left me hard as steel, she made her way over to me, landing between my knees.

"That's a very naughty look in your eye, Ms. Miller," I warned in my best cop voice.

Her hands trailed up the inside of my leg to the waistband of my gym shorts. "That's because you look rather delicious sitting here, Mr. Harrison." And damn—if that look in her eye didn't do it for me, that husky, honeyed voice did. Leah was the total package. Smart, loving, courageous, and determined, all wrapped in a sexy exterior. And she was mine. I let that feeling swell and settle in my chest.

With a sly smirk, she slipped her fingers under the waist band of my shorts and pulled them over my rock-hard erection. "What do we have here? Looks like you need some attention."

She lowered her head and kissed the crown, her hand circling the base of me, lifting me up to meet her hungry lips.

A groan escaped my throat as she took me into her mouth. "Fuck, Leah. That feels amazing."

I ran my fingers into her hair, gripping the loose bun to hold it back so I could see better. She met my gaze with a wicked gleam in her eye and skimmed her teeth up the underside of my cock, then swirled her tongue in some kind of voodoo magic suck-swirl rhythm that had me ready to blow in seconds.

"Shit. Baby, if you don't stop...," I gasped my warning.

She slipped her other hand inside my shorts and cupped my balls, then repeated her magic-spell move. I grunted my approval, barely able to breathe, let alone make coherent words. Then, she slid a finger towards my ass, massaging me in the sensitive space just behind my balls and I exploded in her mouth without warning.

This woman manipulated my body like it was hers to control.

Later, after she'd licked me clean and I'd pulled her up in my arms and snuggled her close, she whispered, "I take it you liked that?"

A deep sigh of satisfaction rumbled through my chest. "I love everything about being with you." She went stiff and I realized what I'd said. Needing to change the subject, because it was too soon for me to be laying out all my cards, I reached over and snagged the resource list I'd made for her.

"While you were getting your stretch on, I made that list for you."

She plucked the paper from my fingers and read through it. She was quiet for a minute, and I could almost see her formulating her plans.

I squeezed her wrist and leaned in to kiss her forehead. "All you can do is try, Leah. Be discreet. Let her know you've got her back. And know that I've got yours. When you are ready to make your move, I will help you."

She lowered the paper and pressed a kiss to my jaw. "Thank you."

"So, this weekend my parents are having a big cookout." The words were out before I could stop them. Surprising myself, I realized that I really wanted her to meet my family. To make this "us" official.

"It's a big annual end-of-summer thing they do, and everyone is invited. I know I probably haven't painted them in the best light. But we're a normal family, with the good, bad, and ugly times. And honestly, it's mostly good times." I paused because I was fucking this up already. "All my friends and family will be there. I'd like for you to go. With me."

"With you?" She shifted to meet my eyes. "As in with you-with you?"

I swallowed, suddenly nervous that she wasn't in the same space as me. That all that we'd shared, every deep emotion that I was feeling, was one-sided, especially because I was falling, hard, and it had only been a matter of days.

I studied her face, tracking every freckle, the laugh lines that radiated from her eyes. I brushed a lock of hair from her forehead and admitted, "Yeah. With me-with me."

She smiled her beautiful smile at me, her eyes growing soft. "I'd love that." She kissed me, and I clung to her mouth like she'd just given me new life, and then I rolled over her to show her how much I loved it too.

Chapter 10

Leah

Waiting to talk to Karen the next day was an exercise in patience. I had no idea how she'd react to me inserting myself into her situation. If she'd feel supported or be offended. I warred with myself all day, questioning whether I was doing the right thing.

I'd been down this road before and had failed tremendously. And if I failed again, the consequences would affect not only the two of us, but possibly this business I shared with Kylie as well. What if her husband got wind that I was onto him? He could end our rental contract and toss us out. I owed it to Kylie to not put our careers in jeopardy.

But even worse, and this was my greater fear, what if he took that anger out on Karen?

Still, I couldn't stand by and choose to take no action. Doing so made me as much to blame as him in my mind.

So when she walked into class, her normal outfit of long sleeves and pants took on new meaning for me. I'd always thought it curious that she was usually covered head to toe, regardless of the weather, but maybe there was more to it. I made up my mind. I found the list of resources that I'd copied onto a blank greeting card. If her husband found it, at least at first glance it would look like a card from a friend. Tucking the card into an envelope with her name on it, I waited until the exact right moment, trusting that instinctually I would know when the time came.

Kylie was in the lobby helping a new client register and Karen was just stepping from the studio room when I caught her.

"Hey, Karen. I have a little something for you." I flipped the card out as nonchalantly as I could, and quickly hid my hands so she wouldn't see them shake.

"What's this?" She tilted her head to the side, a little smile of curiosity peeping out.

"It's nothing much. Just a note because I was thinking of you." I offered her a genuine smile, hiding my nerves.

"That's very sweet, Leah." She flipped the note card over as if to open it.

"Please wait until you are alone." I hurried to stop her from possibly embarrassing us both. "I got really vulnerable with my note, and I'm a little shy about that."

She tapped it against her palm, eyeing me curiously. "Okay. Well thank you, I guess?"

I laughed, feeling all kinds of awkward, willing her to let me own the uncomfortable silence that fell between us.

"I just appreciate you and wanted to share why. That's all."

"Hey, Leah," Kylie called from the front room. "Can you come up here for a minute?"

Karen looked toward the front before shifting her attention back to me. "I was hoping you'd fill me in on seeing you and Mike Harrison at dinner the other night, but I guess this isn't a good time to talk."

I blushed to the roots of my hair, my entire face on fire,

and I couldn't stop the silly smile that sprung up on my face at the mention of his name.

"I guess with that blush, I don't have to wonder how you feel," she said with a smile. "I'm happy for you, Leah. He's a wonderful young man. I've known his family forever." We made our way up the hallway where we paused at the front door. "I hope this means you'll be at his parents' annual barbecue?"

"He asked me just last night."

She smiled at that and turned to leave. "I'll see you there."

Suddenly I wasn't sure if the card had been a good idea or not. But what was done was done. And I definitely wasn't sure of Mike's vow to stand by me, but I'd just have to trust that he'd help me when the time came.

Chapter 11

Mike

"So did you put in for the Fire Marshal position?" Thoren asked, swinging his axe overhead.

We were at his place, a small farmhouse that sat on the knoll of a pasture, working on building up his firewood stack. Firefighter by day with a side job of delivering firewood by the truckload, Thoren had asked me to come help after my shift because he had a delivery of pecan scheduled.

As he split, I hauled and stacked for him. Then we'd switch places, and I would take my turn with the axe.

"Yeah." I grunted under the weight of a large wedge. I dropped the wedge on his cutting base and stepped back while he swung.

"And?"

"I haven't heard anything yet. But I think my chances are good. Unless some outsider comes in and just blows me out of the water, I think Captain Collins wants me for the job."

Thoren swung the axe, the head biting into the wood. Two more blows and the round split neatly in two.

"You ready to leave law enforcement?"

I grabbed a bottle of water, thinking about the question. I would miss being in law enforcement, but I didn't know if that was from a sense of obligation to my family heritage, or because I truly felt called to be a cop.

After a long drink I admitted, "You know, when they first started this task force, I would've said no. But I've enjoyed the work I've done. I like the challenge of it. I like that it's a new position and I can make it my own. I like the investigation and scientific aspect of it. Plus, the coworkers would be a hell of a lot more fun to be with. Hell, I get along better with the guys from your crew than I do my own shift."

The crunch of tires on gravel alerted us to a visitor, and a short while later Nate strolled around the corner of the house.

"Hey, guys. Did I stall long enough for you to get everything done?"

Nate had a California surfer look about him, light brown hair that tended to curl when it got some length. He snagged the axe from Thoren, motioning him to take a break. "What are we talking about?"

"About how Mike put in for that new position."

Nate nodded and gave the axe a swing. "The Fire Marshal position? That's good news, man. You'd be working with us."

"Yeah, that's a definite perk. I just don't know how my family is going to take the news if I get it."

"What do you mean?" Nate asked.

"Mike's whole family has been law enforcement for a couple of generations," Thoren explained.

Nate grunted with his next swing and the log split in

two. "I say go for it. Plus, you'll still get to wear your shiny badge."

Thoren tilted his head and pointed at Nate with the water bottle he held. "Fair point. Now that we've decided your career path, tell me how it's going with the yoga chick."

I couldn't stop the grin from spreading across my face at the thought of her. "She's amazing."

They both moaned in disgust.

"No way," Nate whined. "Thoren, don't tell me Big Bad Mike went and caught feelings."

"I hate to break it to you, young Nate. He's head over heels from the look of it. That goofy grin is only worn by a man who is truly under the spell of the magic pussy." Thoren grinned like he was a fucking genius, and I saw red, my grin quickly dropping to a frown.

"You watch your mouth when you speak of her. Have some respect."

Thoren dropped the joking, smartly zeroing in on the seriousness of my tone.

"I'm fucking serious. She's sweet and kind and everything good. And I'll be damned if I stand by and let you make fun of this thing we have between us, or her for that matter. She's not some piece of ass."

He drew his hands up in surrender. "Easy there, buddy. No harm was meant."

"It was fucking rude though, and you know it."

Thoren and Nate both watched me in stunned silence. I'd never acted this way about a woman before. I'd normally be joking with them and suddenly it hit home how disrespectful an asshole I'd been to every woman I'd ever been involved with.

"I realize that I'm being a one-hundred-percent

hypocrite right now. But I'm telling you. There is something about this woman."

Nate dropped the axe and headed to the back porch. He drew out three beers from the small mini fridge Thoren kept there.

"Here. Drink this. It's all good. Your woman is amazing. We're all a bunch of jerks who think with our dicks. And you're getting a new job."

"Nice try." I shook off Nate's offer, suddenly feeling the need to go prove myself to Leah and feeling wholly unworthy of any attention she might bestow on me.

He waggled the beer in front of me. "Come on, man. I'm sure she's just as amazing as you say she is."

I snagged the beer and took a long swig, letting the icy brew cool my temper.

Thoren made his way to one of the Adirondacks around his fire pit. "So, are you taking her home to meet the fam?"

I nodded. "Yeah, I invited her to the party this weekend."

Thoren whistled low as Nate's eyebrows shot up his forehead. "Whoa...it's that serious? Didn't you just meet her?"

I nodded. "Yeah, but I feel like I've known her forever. We just click. I know it sounds stupid, or foolish, or whatever. I don't know. It's like she sees the real me—there's no bullshit or games. So yeah. She's special and what we have is special."

Silence fell between us as we all seemed to ponder my words. Finally, Thoren lifted his beer in salute. "Here's to hoping that your family doesn't fuck up a good thing then."

And suddenly, a thread of unease rolled through me, because he had a point. I'd had a happy childhood and my family had always been solid, even if sometimes I felt like they never let me grow out of "little brother" status. Hopefully they wouldn't treat her the same way. And if they did, I'd just have to man up and stand up to them once and for all.

Which was a crazy thought. What was it about this woman that had me so tied up that I was ready to forsake my family and give shit to my friends?

Since when had I become the guy that would give up everything that had ever been important to me for someone I'd just met?

And more importantly, what if things didn't work out between us? Then again, what if they did?

Chapter 12

Leah

"Come on, woman. Get a move on! I need a drink already!" Kylie called from my kitchen.

"Hold your horses. I'm almost ready," I called back, adding an extra swipe with the mascara brush. Truth be told, I was nervous and procrastinating like a champ. Tonight was a friends meetup at a bar downtown called The Alamo, and since Mike had already met Kylie, it was more that I was meeting all of his friends for the first time.

I took a last glance in the mirror and gave up.

"Girl, what's that look for?" Kylie said from the doorway.

I shrugged, capping the wand and tossing the tube to my makeup bag. "What if they don't like me?"

"Then they're stupid." She stepped up beside me and met my gaze in the mirror. "Girl, you don't get it. It's their privilege to know you. Besides that, you are my favorite person in the world, and I wouldn't bullshit you. They will love you. And even if they don't, I do, and I'm thinking your fella does too."

She threw an arm over my shoulders and gave me a side hug. "Come on. It's going to be fine."

I swallowed and allowed her to guide me out of the house, to the car, and then inside the bar. Normally I'd be okay. This anxious, flighty bird I'd become wasn't me. I just knew I really liked Mike and wanted to make a good impression on his friends.

I caught his eye almost the second we entered the building. He was already at the bar, surrounded by a group of guys.

"Damn, girl. If those are his friends...we are in for a fun night," Kylie muttered beside me. "That lumbersnack is yummy."

I could almost hear her smacking her lips at the sight of a tall, burly guy in flannel.

"Oh, but wait, there's more. Check out the surfer guy." She gave a low cat call, and I thanked my lucky stars it hadn't been at full volume.

I snorted at Kylie's antics, but still managed to level a stern look at her. "Behave."

She rolled her eyes. "Whatever."

This was our standard interaction when we went out, and I was grateful that she'd understood I was nervous and reminded me of all that I had in my life.

I stepped forward and met Mike's smile with one of my own. He pulled me close, slipping an arm around my shoulders as he dropped a kiss on my cheek. "Hey, beautiful."

"Hey, yourself."

He looked deep in my eyes and his dimple popped out. "Don't be nervous, babe. They're harmless."

Though I was grateful for his reassurance, it didn't mean the nerves evaporated. "That's easy for you to say.

You've known these guys forever. Also, I'd bet you've never been nervous a day in your life."

That wasn't true though. He'd totally been nervous on our first date, and it'd been adorable.

"Plus, you've got that whole..."

He waited for me to finish, but I couldn't. "My whole what?"

"I don't know. Charisma? Man-in-charge vibe? Plus, I mean, look at you."

His eyes twinkled as he pulled me in for a kiss. "How do I look?"

I narrowed my eyes. "You know how you look."

His arms tightened around me as he spoke against my lips, eyes glued to mine. "But I don't know how I look to you."

"Ugh, get a room already." Kylie's voice rang loud and clear. I turned, cheeks scorching hot, to face the man-squad eyeing me with curiosity.

"Guys, this is Leah." Mike sounded proud, and I soaked in the confidence his tone gave me. "Leah, meet Nate Williams." He gestured to the surfer dude. "And this is Thoren Watkins." He swung a hand towards the flannel guy.

I gave them a dorky wave. "Hey, guys."

Thoren gave me a careful once-over, then gave me a brief nod and met Mike's gaze. I knew instantly that he was the one I'd need to impress the most.

Kylie sidled in between the two men, looking like a wild child with her crazy mix of blonde and red hair, and her sequined tank top that read *"Diva."*

"I'm Leah's bestie, Kylie."

Nate said a polite hello and stepped to the bar, motioning to the bartender for a round of drinks. Thoren looked like he'd been smacked in the face though. Kylie left that kind of impression. She was the kind of woman that people either loved or hated instantly. As Thoren's interest lingered on her, I placed him in the first group.

By the second round of drinks, the tension had eased off, and I was laughing at one of Kylie's stories when Mike's lips brushed my ear.

"See? Nothing to worry about. Do you feel better now?"

I nodded but knew full well I still had the meet-the-family hurdle to jump. I pushed that thought aside and took in this vision of Mike in his element with his friends. By the third round, Thoren had chimed in with tales of him and Mike as new friends, and the tricks they'd played on each other in their police versus fire prank wars.

I drank in the way Mike's eyes crinkled around the edges as he laughed. The way he kept an arm looped at my waist, giving me space to move but still touching me. And I hoped that his family liked me because I was falling fast for this man.

Everything was going fine until the group decided to leave one bar and head to another. The second one was a swanky expensive place that had outdoor seating, and a killer acoustic band playing on a small stage. I recognized some of my yoga students among the faces and immediately felt out of place, even though they greeted me with affection.

Across the bar I spotted Karen with a group of her friends, deep in animated conversation. But something about their interaction seemed fake. Richard stood behind her, his back to her, but every once in a while, I'd notice her flinch.

Slipping his hand to the small of my back, Mike leaned

down to my ear. "That's the second time you've tensed up. What gives?"

I turned, trying to come up with an excuse.

He stopped me with a look. "Don't even think of telling me it's nothing."

Mike had proven himself trustworthy so far. Even though I hated to cast my suspicions on people that might be his friends, he'd surely believe me if I confided in him. "Can we find somewhere private to talk?"

Tugging me to an unoccupied corner of the bar patio, he placed himself between me and the crowd, giving my hand a reassuring squeeze.

"What's going on, beautiful?"

I ran a hand over my curls and tried to release some tension with a breath. "You remember our talk the other morning? When you got me those 'resources?'"

He went still. If there was a threat here, he would take care of it. Beyond a shadow of a doubt, this man would stand up for anyone, anytime.

"Yeah."

"I tucked the list into a card and gave it to the woman I thought might need it."

"Okay. That's good."

"But Mike," I dropped to a whisper as I searched his eyes. "They're here, she's here. With him. Tonight. And she's acting weird."

He scanned the bar. "Who?"

"Karen," I mouthed when his eyes met mine, even though there was no one to hear us. Realization dawned, and a myriad of emotions crossed his face as if the idea of one of his parents' friends abusing his wife was unthinkable. And in that moment, I knew I'd been wrong to confide in him and expect him to help when it involved people he knew, and seemingly respected. Especially without any hard evidence.

"Are you sure?"

He might as well have slapped me. Hurt and disbelief warred inside me. I thought he'd take my word. "What happened to 'having my back?'"

"Don't be offended at my question. It's just that I've known most of these people my whole life. And you are making a serious accusation."

I stared at him for a long moment, then straightened my spine. Without another word, I brushed by him and went back to the bar to gather my purse and tell Kylie I'd call her later.

Mike caught up with me at the sidewalk.

"Leah, we need to talk about this."

"No, we don't. You're going to forget I said anything." I should've known better than to try to intervene.

"You're overreacting."

"Don't tell me what I'm doing. At least I'm trying to help someone I believe is in trouble," I snapped.

The red light at the corner forced me to pause, and embarrassment washed over me as I stood there next to Mike. I never should've asked for his help.

His hand latched on to my hand, spinning me to face him. "Babe. It's not that I don't believe you. I'm sorry that my initial reaction made you feel that way. I've just seen too many cases where victims have denied any abuse, and it's easier if there is a witness or physical evidence."

He was right, of course. "But what if she doesn't, or can't, say anything?"

His fingers gripped mine, and he cupped my cheek with his other hand. "Then you are doing the right thing by showing up for her and letting her know help is out there and someone believes her."

The light went through a whole cycle before I admitted to myself that I'd been wrong. Ashamed that I'd taken my frustration out on him, I studied the buttons on his shirt as I said, "You're right and I'm sorry I stormed out. It's just upsetting."

"I know it is." His voice was gentle as he tipped my chin up, forcing me to look at him. "But we'll pay attention and support her if she needs it. Okay?"

Chapter 13

Leah

Mike pulled his truck up to the curb of a lovely ranch house in an established neighborhood. Not a speck of grass was out of place on the perfectly-manicured lawn. Mature rose bushes adorned the flower bed that lined the front of the house, and a crisp, new American flag hung by the stairs to the porch.

"Wow, what a pretty place," I said, wiping my hands on my flowy skirt, super glad I'd chosen it over jeans. Mike had said "casual" when I'd asked what would be appropriate to wear. But further interrogation had revealed that casual to his folks meant khakis and a button down, as opposed to my definition, which was jeans and a t-shirt.

"Wait here," he ordered, climbing out of the truck. I watched him round the hood to open my door.

He seemed a bit on edge, which was doing nothing to ease my nerves. So when my palm met his offered hand, I noticed that both our hands shook slightly.

He stepped back, allowing me space to climb out, and I didn't miss the way he took in the house while blowing out a long breath.

"I'm really nervous," I blurted, my hands twisting the front of my skirt. Mike's attention darted to me.

"It'll be fine."

"Well, you're acting all weird. How am I supposed to trust that?"

He stepped into my space and brushed an errant curl behind my ear, a small smile playing at the corner of his eyes. "You're right, and I'm sorry. I guess I'm nervous too. I've never brought anyone home before."

His finger skimmed my jaw as he gazed deeply into my eyes. "I'm a lucky bastard to have you on my arm."

I focused on his brown eyes, the way the outer edge of his iris faded from the lightest brown to a warm chocolate. I watched the expression in them grow from amused to understanding, to something that looked a lot more precious.

"I hope they like me," I admitted.

He took a step closer, his hand grazing my back as he drew me close. "Baby, I hope they do too. But it doesn't matter if they do or don't. I do. That's all that matters."

My gaze dropped to his lips.

"But if you keep looking at my mouth like you want a taste of me, right here on my parents' front lawn, you won't be meeting them tonight. We'll be sneaking off to do more fun things."

He pressed his hips to mine, demonstrating solid evidence of the effect my gaze was having on him. His eyes grew darker and his voice ragged when he rasped, "Damn, Leah, let's get this over with so we can get on with those more fun things sooner rather than later."

He dropped his lips to mine for a brief but hungry kiss.

Finally, he broke away and dragged me up the sidewalk. I focused on making sure I wasn't breathing too hard when I met his mother for the first time. Surely she'd know with a single look that I was ready to jump her son.

No one greeted us as we walked into the house, which I found odd.

"They're probably all out back," Mike explained as we passed through an open living room. A stone fireplace took up most of the far wall and comfortable-looking leather furniture all faced the hearth, where a large TV hung over the mantle. I paused to admire some family photos on a narrow table behind the couch.

There were several photos of an older version of Mike with one arm around an attractive woman and one around a young man in a dirty baseball uniform. The kid had to be Mike's brother, while a younger Mike stood to the side of them, looking like he didn't want to be in the picture. They all smiled brightly except for Mike, whose expression wasn't exactly sullen, but it didn't shine with happiness either.

"That was after my brother won the state championship game his senior year."

I picked up the photo and tilted my head to study the picture.

"You weren't happy for him?"

Mike took the photo and studied it a second before placing it back carefully and taking my hand. "Yeah, I was happy for him. It was just a bad time for me. I was kind of acting like a jerk."

Realization dawned. "This was around the time you won your state title, wasn't it?"

Mike didn't answer, just gave a single bob of his head.

I didn't have to ask. I knew there wouldn't be a single family picture of his special day. My heart went out to the boy who needed love and didn't feel like he received it. I slipped my arm around his waist and leaned into him, wishing I could take away that small hurt.

"It doesn't matter." His voice sounded strained. "I still got the medal." His hand drifted up to my shoulder where he gave me a squeeze. "And I made the local paper." I looked up to his forced grin. "That's one awkward picture that I hope has been long since buried."

He was teasing, but it sounded fake.

I took pity on him. "Okay, Running Man. You ready to go face the music and then get out of here? I'm interested in learning more about those 'fun things' you mentioned earlier."

Chapter 14

Mike

The momentary flash of that teenage memory left me in a shitty state of mind. I shook it off as the blip of time that it was and took Leah at her word. The sooner we got done with this shindig, the sooner we could get to the more important part of the night. Namely, me being buried inside her until neither of us could see straight.

I pushed through the French doors and led her out onto the deck that overlooked the back yard full of my parents' friends. Overly loud laughter boomed from the grill area where a circle of men had congregated. The ladies were all balancing wine glasses on their knees, seated around the fire pit.

And across the porch, my parents huddled around my brother, who had his arm slung around an attractive brunette.

"You gotta be fucking kidding me," I gritted the words out. "Leave it to Robbie to bring home his flavor of the month on the same night I bring my woman home for the first time."

Leah's small hand squeezed mine, bringing me back to the present, and reminding me of my goal–meet the parents, get Leah home. So I sucked up my pride and led her right into the fire.

"Hey Ma, Dad."

At my voice, my mother turned away from the brunette, her eyes going wide with surprise. "Mikey, you made it."

Fuck, I hated that nickname.

"I do every year, Ma," I mumbled bending to receive her hug.

"I know you do, but it's still wonderful that you're here," she said, patting my back. "And who is this?" Ma released me, her attention shifting to Leah.

"This is my girlfriend, Leah." Bless her heart, Leah didn't miss a beat at my declaration, she just stuck out her hand and smiled.

"Hello, Mrs. Harrison, it's a pleasure to meet you."

"It's lovely to meet you," Ma said enthusiastically, turning to my dad. "This is my husband, Thomas and this" —Ma paused dramatically—"is Mike's brother, Robbie."

Robbie lifted a hand at Leah, then gave me a bear hug, thumping me hard on the back. It didn't escape my notice that he didn't bother to introduce his friend.

Introductions done, I made our excuses and pulled Leah over to the bar table set up especially for the evening. I was reaching for our beers when I felt Leah stiffen beside me.

"What's wrong?" I asked, following her gaze. Nothing seemed amiss, so I turned back to find her leaning closer to me.

"Nothing," she said, with a shake of her head. "I'm just being ridiculous."

I knew she was lying, but let it ride, tamping down the

feeling that she was hiding something from me. She'd tell me later.

"Let's go find some food, make our rounds, and get the heck out of here."

And oh, what a wonderful plan that was. Then my father chose that moment to corner us.

"Mike, how are things at the station?"

"Good."

Awkward silence passed between us for a beat, then Leah spoke up, slipping her hand into mine. "Did Mike tell you about the new position he's applied for?"

Bless her innocent soul. Leah had no idea that she'd just detonated a land mine, right in the middle of my parents' party.

"No, he didn't." Dad said with a smile at her. But I knew what was coming. He'd hate that I was moving out of law enforcement. "What position is that?"

He directed his question at me, but Leah piped up to answer, her voice high and nervous. "It's an inspector thing at the fire department."

All pretense of pleasantness dropped from Dad's face. "Is that so?"

And damn if I didn't want to rewind and erase the previous thirty seconds. Obviously realizing that Dad wasn't as excited about the new job prospect as we were, Leah backpedaled. "Well, it's not a sure thing. But I'm proud of him for putting in for it. And the guys all say he'll do an excellent job." She turned wide eyes to me, almost begging me to step in and put an end to the awkward conversation.

Just as I opened my mouth, my mom rang a bell and called for everyone's attention. Dad gave me a look that promised more conversation about the topic, then offered Leah a tight smile.

"That's my cue," he said and left without another word, passing through the crowd to stand at Mom's side.

"We just wanted to thank everyone for coming out for our annual end-of-summer cookout. It's wonderful to see you all." She paused for dramatic effect. "This year I'm so thrilled to have both my boys here." She smiled at me, then Robbie. "And we have some wonderful news to share. Our Robbie has just passed his Lieutenant's test and been awarded a promotion."

At that news, Dad reached over and slapped my brother on the back, leaving his hand clamped proudly on his shoulder. Mom went on to personally thank several of their longtime friends for making the drive. The familiar old dread of not meeting their expectations washed over me and I was once again that teenage kid glowering in the family photo.

"And thanks to Karen and Richard for the lovely donation of wine for this evening." Mom thrust her glass high towards the couple. Richard saluted with his glass before tossing the whole thing back. Beside him, Karen stood in polite acceptance of mom's words, looking like she'd rather not be the center of attention.

Beside me, Leah went still, and I knew it was because of what she thought was going down between those two. I ran a hand through my hair. This whole night was circling the drain, and all I wanted to do was go back to the beginning and never set foot in my parents' house.

Chapter 15

Leah

The party was in full swing in short order. I'd lost Mike to a group of men talking baseball, so I made my way to a chair just on the outskirts of a group of ladies. Far enough away from the crowd that I wouldn't be obligated to talk to people, but close enough that I could keep an eye on Karen, because I hoped that maybe I'd get a chance to talk to her.

On the other side of the large patio, Karen stood with a half-full wine glass in her hand. Behind her, a loud laugh boomed. She was cool as a cucumber, but I caught the tiny flinch she failed to control, and realized her husband was the one with the big laugh. I'd not seen this side of them. My business relationship was always controlled and matter-of-fact. Seeing them in a different light, I wondered if maybe I'd misjudged this situation.

Richard boomed in laughter again, tossing back another drink, and Karen took a step away.

I was lost in thought, running through my options of how I could discreetly engage in conversation with her, when two large hands landed on the back of the chair across from me.

"Leah." Mike's deep voice caressed my ears. "You disappeared."

He rounded the chair, lowering into it before bracing his elbows on his knee and leaning toward me. "I'm ready to get on to the rest of our evening. How about you?

"Michael," his mother crooned, approaching us with a flamboyant spreading of her arms. "Isn't it excellent news about Robbie?"

Mike huffed a laugh. "Yeah, Ma. It's great."

"There you are. We've been looking all over for you," a familiar deep voice called across the patio.

I looked up to find Thoren and Nate had arrived. Both reached Mike's mom and gave her a perfunctory hug. "Hi, Mrs. H. Sorry we're late."

"Thoren, Nathaniel. I'm so pleased you could make it."

Mike blew a breath out, obviously frustrated with the interruption of our not-conversation, but he pushed to his feet and shook hands with the newcomers. Then he turned and asked, "You need anything, babe? I'm going to get the guys a beer."

Panic flared in me. Surely, he wouldn't leave me with his mother.

I shook my head no, unable to form words against the rising tide of my frustration and watched him lead his friends away. Why couldn't I speak up for myself? For anyone? Why was he leaving me here alone with this woman when we'd just met? This night was not going well.

Mike's mom sidled around to perch on the edge of the cushioned chair across from me. She seemed pleasant enough, so I tried to tamp down my irritation at the whole evening and put on a brave face. Over her shoulder, I watched Richard join the group of women and lean in to speak directly into Karen's ear.

Around us, the party was going full tilt. Music was cranked up so loud I couldn't think.

"So how did you and Mikey meet?" his mother asked, nearly yelling over the noise.

I focused my attention on her, keeping Karen in my peripheral. "We met when he came to do an inspection at my yoga studio."

"Oh, interesting. That must be the place Karen was speaking so highly of." Behind Mrs. Harrison, Karen's head turned at the mention of her name, but was quickly diverted by her husband. From the corner of my eye, I watched as his large hand gripped her above the elbow and he led her farther into the yard, away from the group.

"What kind of inspection was he doing?"

I focused back on Mrs. Harrison. "The building next door had caught on fire previously, and he was doing an investigation of it. He came to inspect my place and make a pre-fire plan for our building." Did she not know what her son did?

"Oh, yes. That task force thing he mentioned. You know, we were so disappointed that he didn't choose to go to the same department as Robbie and his father and grandfather before him." She sighed dramatically.

"But how exciting was it that Robbie passed his test?" Her hands fluttered enthusiastically, and I wanted to just grab them and hold her still.

"Did Mike tell you about the opportunity he has?" I tried to interject, but she spoke right over me.

She flipped her hand dismissively. "Maybe Mikey will

reconsider once he hears how much more money Robbie will be making."

I sat in stunned disbelief as once again I was disregarded. But much worse, she also disregarded her own son. And I really wanted to tell her to stop with the stupid nickname.

I was rescued by the golden child himself. "Mom, I've gotta head out. Gretchen has an early call in the morning."

"Oh, that's too bad, sweetheart. I was just getting to know Mikey's friend." She rose, going all the way on her tiptoes to press a kiss to her son's cheek.

I didn't want to make nice with Mike's brother, or his mother for that matter. I was ready to find Mike and get the heck out of Dodge.

In the distance, a male voice rising in anger caught my attention, and I turned in time to glimpse the edge of Karen's skirt disappearing around the corner of the house.

Dread pooled in my stomach. What if he had found my note? What if he was dragging her off to hurt her again?

It didn't make sense that he would do something around all these people, but the man had been slamming drinks from the moment I'd first noticed him.

I needed to find Mike. It was obvious that Mr. Lindell was well-liked in this crowd. I'd need proof, or a convincing argument about my suspicions at the least. But I didn't want to wait around and take a chance on Karen getting hurt by taking the time to look for Mike. I was on my own.

"Excuse me," I murmured to no one in particular, and took off toward the area I'd last seen Karen.

"Leah!" Mike's voice rang from behind me. I didn't pause, hustling off the patio and through the yard. I heard his footsteps seconds before his hand clasped my elbow, pulling me to a stop.

"Let me go!" I demanded, jerking my arm away from him. "She's in trouble."

His whole demeanor changed. He straightened, head swiveling in the direction we'd been heading. "The Lindells?"

I responded by sprinting around the corner, Mike hot on my heels.

He passed me when I drew up short at the corner of the house. Richard was at the edge of the yard with his back to us, but I could see he had Karen by the arm. He gave her a vicious shake as tears streamed down her face.

Mike sprinted but was too late. Richard let loose with a back handed blow that sent Karen sprawling, crying out in pain. Mike growled and dove, taking the man down. Richard fought back, throwing a punch that Mike quickly blocked by grabbing Richard's arm and using it as leverage to wrestle him to submission. The whole scene lasted a split second, but it felt like a lifetime.

Mike braced a knee in Richard's back, keeping his arm twisted up behind him.

I raced to kneel by Karen, wrapping my arms around the sobbing woman. "Shh, it's okay. We're here."

Richard let loose a string of curses as Mike pulled him to stand and pressed him against the brick wall of the house.

"What in the hell is going on out here? Michael, get your hands off Richard! Son, you don't treat my guests that way," Mike's dad boomed.

"I do when I see the bastard hitting his wife. Or did you forget that assault is illegal?" Mike barked, eyes flashing at his father.

The party guests formed a wall of onlookers, and I huddled over Karen, trying to protect her from their view. I had to get her somewhere that she wasn't a spectacle.

Thoren, Nate, and Robbie muscled their way through the crowd, taking Mike's place. Robbie looked at Mike. "I've got him until a squad can get here."

I ushered Karen to her feet and led her inside, following Mike to a small powder room. I lowered the toilet lid and directed her to sit so I could tend her cut lip. Her cheek was bright red where Richard had hit her, but what concerned me most was the way she held herself. The confident strong woman from my class was in there, hanging on to her dignity by a thread.

Mike's gaze met mine over Karen's bowed head, remorse shining brightly in his eyes. I steeled myself from the onslaught of emotions that threatened to overtake me.

"I'll go grab some ice and a first aid kit.".

With his exit, Karen seemed to let go, curling into herself as a sob rocked her body. Stepping around her, I closed the door to afford her some privacy, and pulled her head to my belly. She made no move, other than to lean her weight into me, but I felt her trembles as surely as if they were mine.

Smoothing her hair, I bent over her and just held her, not knowing what to say, what to do.

Mike returned with the ice and a small kit, then left us alone.

"Karen, let me take care of you," I whispered to the top of her head.

Sitting back so I could place the ice on her cheek, she sniffled and whispered back, "Thank you, Leah. I wish I could say I don't know how this happened, but I think you'd know that was a lie." Her voice broke.

"Stop, Karen. My only role here is to care for you and try to find you some help. Did you read my card?"

She shook her head. "I was scared to. I knew you had

suspicions, and I didn't want to know what you thought of me. So I avoided it. But I still have it."

"Good. There is a list of resources for you in there. People who can help you."

Outside the door, Mike's mom and several of the other ladies were speaking loudly. Mike's low voice rumbled in return. He must've been standing guard, protecting us.

She allowed me to put ointment on her cut and finally met my eyes. "I didn't think anyone would ever believe me that he could be a monster. But you took one look at me and knew. You took a great risk doing that, knowing he could retaliate by terminating your lease if you said anything."

He still could and probably would, but I offered her a small smile, despite my worry. "I can find another place to rent." And that was the truth of it. Kylie would understand, and we would start over.

More voices sounded outside the door, followed by a knock as Mike cracked the door. "Karen, do you feel like speaking with an officer to press charges?"

Her watery gaze met mine.

"Do you want someone to go with you?" I whispered. "It sounds like you have some friends out there. I'm sure they're all concerned."

With a nod, she pulled herself together and rose, wrapping me in a hug. "Thank you, Leah."

I opened the door, bumping into Mike. "She's ready."

He was in full protector mode as he ushered us to the dining room, where two other officers waited. I asked Karen if she wanted me to stay, but she declined. Once she began giving her statement to the officers, Mike's hand hit the small of my back.

"Come with me, please."

He was all politeness and chivalry. I could tell he

wanted to talk, but my feelings were so raw and I was so on edge, I didn't know if I could handle anything more. "I'd like to go home."

"I know. After you give your statement as a witness, I'll take you."

I gave my statement to the officers with Mike standing guard over me. Once I was released, the weight of the evening's events bore down on me. And I was confused. Because although he'd not wanted to believe me at first, Mike had stepped up quickly, and then he'd not left my side.

He'd had my back.

I needed to acknowledge that, but I was so hollow and spent from all the drama, I couldn't decide where to start. So when he led me to the kitchen and placed a glass of water in front of me, I just stared at it, looking for answers in ripples of the clear liquid. The awkward tension between us was too much.

"I wish this whole night had never happened," I whispered. "I hate this drama."

Mike sunk to the stool beside me, bracing a heel on the rung, his knee brushing my leg. He spiked his fingers through his hair "I know, and we still need to talk." He didn't look like the charming, happy man that walked into my yoga studio. This was a dark, serious side of him that I hadn't yet seen.

"I'm so sorry. I left you feeling like you were in this battle alone. I said I'd be there for you, and even though it was for a split second, I let you down. I promise you, it'll never happen again."

I paused to absorb his words and tried to sort through the muddle of feelings swirling through me. I was feeling strung out, raw, and angry. All I wanted was for us to leave, and find our way back to the innocent, blissful space we'd been in before everything went to hell.

Before I could respond, the back door opened, and Mike went rigid. "Mikey, oh my god, what happened?" Mike's mom burst through like a whole hour hadn't already passed.

And just like that, our evening took another turn.

Chapter 16

Mike

My folks had shit timing.

"Son, explain," my dad barked, following my mom into the room.

I bristled, unable to temper the red haze that washed over me with his bullshit attitude. "Your buddy Richard, or maybe we should just call him Dick, backhanded his wife."

"That's a serious accusation, son." His hands landed on his hips, and he lowered that direct gaze that had me scrambling as a kid. It wasn't lost on me that he'd used the same words I had with Leah. Suddenly, I had a taste of what she'd felt, and it rankled.

But I wasn't a kid anymore, and he wasn't going to just act like nothing had happened. "It's the truth." I barked back. "Leah had been suspecting it. Thank God she was watching and saw him drag her away." I shuddered at the possibilities of what could have happened had Leah not been there, or worse, if Richard had turned his violence on Leah.

Dad kept his interrogation going. "But did you actually see anything before you tackled the man?"

He just couldn't take me at my word. He always had to question my ability and motive. I snorted in disgust. "If I'd been Robbie, you'd be clapping me on the back. Tell me, Dad. Do you not want to believe that your friend could be abusive to his wife? Or have you been ignoring it?" I clenched my fist against the truth I wanted to spout and the fear that maybe he wasn't the cop I'd always believed him to be. I knew he loved me, but times like this, when he showed his distrust in my judgment, felt like a knife to the heart. All I wanted was to make him proud. It seemed like I never would.

"Mike was right behind me the whole time. So yes, he did see the strike." Leah's razor-sharp reply cut through the tension. I glanced over because that sharp tone didn't mesh with the Leah I'd known the short time we'd been together.

Dad's eye's narrowed on her briefly, but he gave a nod of affirmation. Even if he didn't want to, it seemed like he was coming to terms with the situation.

"Thank goodness the both of you were there then," Mom said, relief in her voice. "Come on. We need to get back out there. We do still have other guests here."

Mom ushered us back outside to find most of the partygoers had made their exit. The remaining friends gathered around the fire pit and conversation settled into normal topics, like baseball playoff races and upcoming football seasons. It felt weird and unsettling that the whole drama with Karen and Richard was just...forgotten. Or at the very least, put into the box of things-we-don't-discuss.

"...just so proud of Robbie for going for that promotion." My mother's voice penetrated my thoughts. She looked to my dad. "Right, honey?"

"Now if we can just convince Michael to follow in the

family tradition, all of the Harrisons will have been on the force at APD."

Same shit, different day. "Dad, we've had this discussion before. I don't want to work in Atlanta."

"I don't understand why not. It's your heritage."

I fought an eyeroll. "It's just not me. I like where I am." For the most part.

"That's it then? You don't want something better? You're just...settling?"

He was like a record with only one song on it.

Dad had never forgiven me for choosing track. In his eyes, track wasn't a "real" sport. His view was that I'd settled for running track when I could've done something more spectacular, like football, baseball, or even soccer. And just like he had his ideas about what a real sport was, he also had ideas about what a real police department was.

Mom intervened by placing a hand on Dad's arm. "Honey, don't start this. I can't deal with anymore turmoil this evening. I'm out of wine." She put a hand to her forehead, feigning exhaustion and sinking to a nearby stool, drawing a chuckle from the circle around us.

I knew damn well she'd paid a party planner. I loved my mother, but she was overly dramatic, and tonight those antics grated on my last nerve.

"Yeah Dad, Michael couldn't help it he was a wormy little joker and didn't grow until he hit college," Robbie piped in, shooting me his trademark shit-eating grin. The one he'd teased me with my whole life. Normally, I could take his ribbing, but tonight I was done with the drama.

Thoren and Nate laughed uncomfortably at the joke. They'd heard this all before, the joking that went a little too far. And even though it got on my nerves, the ribbing would eventually stop and they'd find something else to make fun of. I opened my mouth to ask why Robbie was still there, when we all thought he'd left.

"Stop it," Leah hissed, her soft, steady voice cutting through the awkward chuckles like a bomb detonating. All laughter ceased. I looked over to find her standing, back rigid and fists clenched, glowering at the entire group. Her glare blistering those who'd been laughing.

"You should be ashamed of yourselves. If anything, this evening has taught us that we should be aware of our words and actions. To be kind to people because you never know what they are going through."

Her attention turned to my parents. "You should be proud of Michael for taking on new projects, protecting the very community you chose to raise your family in. Yet here you are, belittling the choices he's made."

"Now wait a minute," my mother stood, hackles raised. "No one is belittling him. We love both our boys. Who do you think you are young lady?"

"You do?" Leah aimed her fiery gaze back at my mom. "That's hard for me to believe. I've seen your family photos. I've noticed how your family poses in them, with Michael on the outskirts. You have all the championship baseball pictures of Robbie and even Mr. Harrison from his days of high school proudly displayed on your wall."

I didn't realize she'd noticed so much, but obviously I'd underestimated my woman.

"But not a single picture of Mike showing off his accomplishments."

"No one was there to take the picture!" my father said defensively.

Leah looked between him and my mother. "Exactly my point." Her quiet words hung in the silence because really, there was nothing they could respond with.

"You should be proud of the man he is." Her hushed voice vibrated with intensity. "You should be proud that he's taking on new roles and challenges. That he chose a career where he could make a difference in the world, and still satisfy your family legacy. Even if that legacy's not what he really enjoys."

Leah dropped her truth bombs and looked over at me, standing like a coward, hiding behind her. I felt the heat of her words and saw the depth of her emotion and knew that I'd been a fool in that split second of hesitation I'd shown when she told me her suspicions about the Lindells.

She hadn't hesitated to take a stand and have my back when I needed it. I hadn't even had to say anything to her. She just stood up for me, somehow knowing that somewhere deep down, their words were like fists to the face of that little boy who'd been dragged along behind his older, better brother.

My beautiful, strong woman came in with stealth and handed my family their asses, all with such dignity and grace. And now she turned those gorgeous eyes on me, wide and shining. I didn't hesitate. I went to her, placing a hand on her back, pulling her to the safety of my arms. No doubt my family would have something to say in response. I'd be the shield that protected her.

I raked a last glance around the room. "Let's get the fuck out of here."

* * *

We pulled up in front of Leah's house after a silent car ride. Her reaction, both to seeing Karen being attacked and going through the drama with my family, was now silence. We'd been on one hell of a roller coaster all evening.

I killed the engine and dropped my hands to my lap, searching for the words that would ease this tension and make things right between us again.

I looked over at Leah, sitting proudly in her seat, eyes fixed out the front window, throat working like she was trying not to cry.

"You were amazing tonight." That got her attention and she finally turned to me.

"How can you say that? I didn't get to Karen before she got hurt, and then I blew up all over your family. Everyone probably hates me now."

Yeah, she was needlessly beating herself up.

I laid my hand over her balled fists. "No one hates you, sweetheart. You didn't do anything wrong with my family, you just put them in their place. Gave them something to think about. They'll have a think on it, and we'll discuss it in a couple of days, and everything will be fine."

I squeezed her hands as I made my point. "And even if things got out of hand with Karen, I'm betting it's the last time. But more than that, you showed her she has support, that there are people willing and wanting to help her. And as much as it pains me to say this, if things hadn't exploded the way they had tonight, I don't know that she would've had the courage to ask for help. But the choice was taken away from her because he chose to do what he did in the middle of a party where there were witnesses. Because of who he is, people would doubt the situation." I swallowed thickly. "I know I did, and in the process, I hurt you."

She watched our hands, then eased hers away.

"Don't do that," I pleaded. "Don't pull away from me."

I didn't reach for her again but took solace that she didn't immediately reach for the door handle.

"Look, I know we're brand new. But from the moment I

laid eyes on you, I knew there was something special about you, and about us. We have a connection." I studied her profile, the way the streetlamp backlit her features. "I know you can feel it," I whispered.

Her eyes closed, and her throat bobbed as she swallowed.

"I know you feel responsible for what happened with Karen. But you didn't backhand her. And what happened with your friend...you weren't the cause of that either. You didn't throw the punches. You were trying to help and tonight, you did."

A tear leaked from her eye, trailing down her cheek like a glittering diamond. My heart clenched at the sight. "Baby, I'm so sorry that I hesitated, and that I hurt you by doing so. It kills me to see you beating yourself up over this, and it kills me that I added to whatever it is that's causing those tears."

Her head bowed, and her small fists clenched again, like she was fighting a war within herself, and I couldn't do anything to help her.

"What's going through your head? Talk to me. Please," I whispered.

Long moments passed while I waited until finally, she looked up and met my eyes, and my heart fell to my stomach.

Chapter 17

Leah

I f I'd had any idea of how the night would go, I would've suggested that Mike and I make an appearance at his folks' place and then retreat to somewhere safe where we could be alone and happy together.

But the evening hadn't gone like that.

And now, here we were with me causing more drama. And it so wasn't me.

I looked up to find Mike fixated on me, concern written all over his handsome face.

His heartfelt apology hadn't fallen on deaf ears. "Thank you for apologizing. And I'll try to let go of some of my anxiety over tonight, but it might take some time and work."

He shifted in his seat. "So where does that leave us?"

I was confused by his question. "What do you mean?"

"Where do things stand with us?"

He sounded worried. Could it be that he thought I'd just end it now? Surely not. But then again, when had anyone ever done the work to make him feel important? He was used to being set aside, whether he realized it or not.

And suddenly my actions toward him the whole

evening made me cringe. I'd been treating him like crap, withholding attention, pulling away. I'd even considered that a relationship with him wasn't worth the effort. Of course he would be feeling that and wonder where things stood between us.

I reached out and cupped his cheek, pulling him toward me to place a soft kiss on his lips. "You and I have some deep work to do. But I hope that we can do it together."

He pulled back and met my eyes. "Does this mean...?"

I swiped my thumb across the stubble of his jaw and admitted, "I don't know what you think it means, but for me, it means that I want to learn and grow, and try to be a better person...with you. I want to show you all the ways I think you are amazing, and how much I appreciate the man you are. I want to support you in your new adventures and be the solid foundation that believes in you."

His hand wrapped around my wrist, his thumb sliding across my pulse, igniting little sparks across my skin.

I kissed him and continued, "I want you to teach me that I don't have to carry the weight of the world. That it's okay to do my best and accept that not everything is my fault."

His hand on my wrist tightened, his heated gaze searching mine. "I want to tell you all the little things I appreciate about you. How considerate and loving you are, even to those who don't always deserve it. I want to show you every day how I'm falling for you."

Then his lips were on mine, and he was pulling me close in the hottest, most soul-searching kiss of my life.

"Fuck," he breathed, pulling away. "I need to get you inside."

He tugged me across the yard and slammed the front door behind us, then immediately pushed me back against it. In a flurry of hands, clothes dropped to the floor, both mine and his. A condom was slid on and I was hoisted up with my back to the door as he sank inside me in one stroke.

A moan ripped from my throat. He felt so good, so right. He drove into me with long, deep strokes. Every thrust let me know that I was his and he was mine. Our bodies proved what our hearts knew. We were meant for each other. With every cry and every moan, he drove harder, faster, deeper, until we both exploded.

Later, while we both tried to catch our breath, he looked deep in my eyes and whispered, "Fuck, I love you."

My heart clenched because a part of me thought the words were too soon. But a deeper part of me had recognized him as my soulmate from the moment I'd laid eyes on him. So I kissed him back, pouring all of my heart, every tender emotion, every fierce desire, everything that was me into that kiss.

I pulled away enough to catch my breath and whispered against his lips, "I love you, too."

Chapter 18

Mike

"Hi, sweetheart." Leah smiled at me from behind the check-in desk as I walked into Blue Lotus.

Just like the first time I'd met her, her smile hit me square in the chest and made it hard to breathe for a second.

"Hey, babe."

She rounded the desk and walked straight into my arms. "This is a nice surprise. What are you doing here?"

I didn't want to be a total pussy and admit that I was nervous and needed to see her to settle those nerves. "I can't stop by and see my woman in the middle of the day, for no reason at all?"

With her head on my chest and her arms around me, my nerves started to settle so I squeezed tighter. I needed to bottle this peacefulness I felt when I was with her and carry it with me always. I pressed my lips to her arm, inhaling the strength this woman gave me. Before she'd come into my life, I'd thought I had it all. How wrong I'd been. My life had been empty before her.

She eased back and gazed at me with eyes that saw

straight to my soul. "Well, of course you can visit anytime. But today isn't just any day, is it?"

I swallowed thickly and managed, "No, it's not."

Today they were supposed to be naming who would take the new Fire Marshal position. And I'd come to the point where I wanted it so badly that it made me tense and anxious. A couple days ago, Leah had hounded me about why I'd been so on edge until I'd finally admitted what was bothering me.

"Well, whatever happens, it will be okay." Her arms tightened around me, and she pecked my cheek. "But I hope they're smart enough to name you."

From my pocket, my cell phone rang. My heart skipped a beat when I pulled it out and read the caller ID.

"I love you," Leah vowed and released me to answer the call.

I took a fortifying breath. "This is Mike."

"Mike, this is Mac Collins."

"Hey, Captain. How's it goin'?" I reached for Leah and gripped her hand.

"I won't beat around the bush." Mac's gruff voice paused, and my heart thumped in anticipation. "I'm proud to let you know that due to your skills and talent on the task force, the powers-that-be have proven that sometimes they don't have their heads up their asses and they've selected you to be the new Fire Marshal. Congratulations, Harrison. Welcome to the fire department."

A massive wave of relief and joy rolled through me. "Thank you, Captain Collins. I look forward to working with you." Understatement of the year.

We made plans to meet in the coming weeks and I hung up and delivered the news to an ecstatic Leah.

My phone blew up with messages. Thoren, Nate, even

Big Mo must have known and been waiting on pins and needles for Mac to make his announcement because they all texted me at once, congratulating me and welcoming me to the department.

I sent out a note in my family group message, and felt my heart expand as my mom and dad sent congratulations. We'd had a tearful reconciliation, and though my dad didn't like that I was choosing a different route, he was finally coming around to the idea and was supportive. Robbie gave me shit as usual, but I could tell he was happy for me.

Somewhere along the way, I'd realized that no matter what my parents thought about this new role, I was excited. And my excitement had finally been enough to win them over. For the first time in a long time, I felt like I had a support team around me. And with Leah by my side, I was ready to face whatever the future held.

The End

Want to see Nate fall head over heels for his special lady? Keep reading for a sneak peak of Burn Point! Ready to dive in now? You can download your copy here!

Get Burn Point here!

Also by Rae Fields

Nate and Jordan
Burn Point

Thoren and Kylie
Flash Point

Mac and Liv - Coming July 2024
Anchor Point

Acknowledgments

This adventure I'm embarking on wouldn't happen without some amazing people in my life. To my BBG- Big Bald Guy, thank you for your endless love and support, for answering my technical questions and for being my ride or die for the past twenty-nine years. To my amazing boys and their sweet wives- thank you for believing in me and encouraging me to chase my dreams. To my bestie, Shawna- thanks for giving me the nudge to hit submit, and for being my loudest cheerleader. To Mia- thank you for your patience, your advice and support. I know I'm a needy bitch. To my HEA crew and 6 a.m. squad- thanks for showing up, brainstorming, critiques, challenges, accountability, and moral support - you guys rock. And to Jessica- we've come a long way lady, and this is just the beginning of our adventure! This new career wouldn't be happening without your guidance and advice, and your unwavering belief in me. I appreciate the community you've built, the classes, the resources...but mostly, all the times you've answered my panicked messages and talked me off a ledge of despair. You're the best!

And if you've made it this far, thank you reader, for taking a chance on this baby author.

About the Author

Rae Fields is beginning her publishing adventure and hopes you'll come along for this journey. She feels weird talking about herself in third person and hopes you'll join her newsletter and socials where she can just talk to you, and not feel weird about it.

Find all my links and join my newsletter at

www.raefields.com

or use this QR code, to keep up with all things Rae!

www.ingramcontent.com/pod-product-compliance
Lightning Source LLC
Chambersburg PA
CBHW030148010826
48973CB00002B/780